THE RUNAWAY

A CONTEMPORARY REVERSE HAREM ROMANCE
(SAVAGE MOUNTAIN MEN)

MIKA LANE

BE THE FIRST TO KNOW...

Want more heat, heart,
and bad boys who know what they're doing?
Join my list and I'll send the steam straight to your inbox,
starting with a deliciously naughty story:

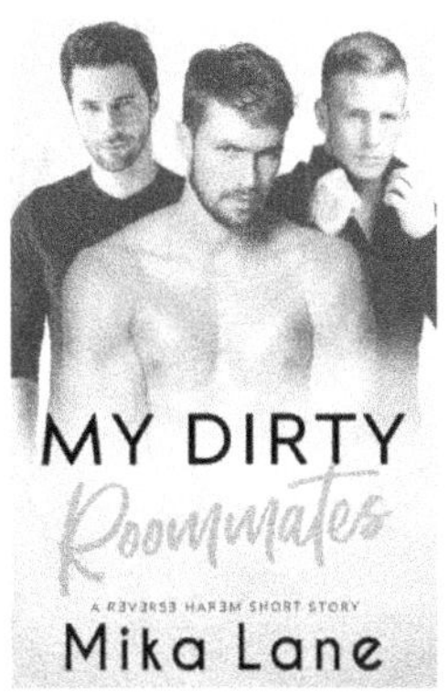

1

CHRISTIAN

"Dude, that is some serious *FUCK YOU* money," I said, looking at my business partner, Red, in the shitty little South American café where we sat, trying to cool off from the intense tropical heat with cold beers.

The other guys, Dutch and Victor, didn't seem so sure.

Dutch leaned back in a chair dwarfed by his six-foot-seven-inch frame, stressing the legs to the limit of their capacity to bear weight. "Speaking for myself, I have all the *fuck you* money I'm gonna need in this lifetime."

He had a point. We all had enough *fuck you* money, if you wanted to be honest about it.

Victor, his ever-present wool cap pulled to his eyebrows in spite of the warm day, tried to explain. "I think what Red's saying, Dutch, is that they can't do the job without you."

"So we're a fucking charity, now?" Dutch asked, rolling his eyes. "We're taking jobs cuz we're nice guys? I'm not sure I can put my life on the line for something like that."

Everyone thought about that.

Looking at his hands, Victor continued, "I know taking jobs is about money. If you don't need the money, why would you take the jobs? The work is dirty and dangerous. But what I hear Red saying is that this would be the last one, and that it would be extremely lucrative."

"I don't know, man," Dutch said, shaking his head. "We just finished *this* job. I just want to get stateside and back on the mountain. De-stress a little, you know?"

"Well, think about it," Red said, scanning the dusty street.

I knew that look of his. In about five seconds flat, he would have assessed every person, car, building, and stray dog within a hundred yards.

No matter what our contacts told us, he always kept an eye out. It was what kept him alive, and the best of the best.

It was what made us *all* the best of the best.

And earned us a shit-ton of money.

The drawback to our work came at the steep price of going through life always looking over your shoulder. Sometimes the people we'd worked with, and sometimes against, had a hard time leaving jobs behind. They'd pop up just when you least expected it. Not good.

The hardest part, though, was putting it all aside when we *weren't* on a job, like having to deal with the adrenaline flood every time someone looked at you the wrong way. And fighting the urge to kill everyone who pissed you off.

But hey, controlling those urges was part of what made us successful. Lesser operatives gave in to the horrors of committing extreme violence against other human beings. Not us.

"Christ, that was a long-ass flight," Dutch groaned, scanning the diner where we could finally get an American burger for the first time in weeks.

The good old scanning. It never stopped.

"Sure was. This travel shit is getting old." My phone vibrated in my pocket. Victor and Red were back on Savage Mountain, the place we called home. Dutch and I would be heading up there as soon as we got our comfort food fix. It was sort of a post-job ritual for the two of us, one of the few exceptions to our rules.

We four never traveled together. Not even in pairs,

usually. There was too high a risk of being seen, of being too big a target. But with this trip, the only way out of the shithole where we'd been working was one measly flight a day. Victor and Red had left the day before us. Dutch and I followed twenty-four hours later.

I looked around the truck stop diner, perusing the scene as I'd been taught so long ago, and which by now was second nature. Besides the diner staff, there were eleven men of all shapes and sizes, but mostly pasty and overweight. That's what trucking did to you, sitting on your ass all day long. I didn't envy those guys, not one bit. It was a hard, lonely life.

And unhealthy as hell by the evidence that surrounded me.

But there was one thing strangely out of place.

A woman. And not the woman behind the counter, slinging hash.

A Greyhound bus had just pulled into the stop, spilling a handful of bedraggled travelers who were after a smoke, a bathroom break, or some shitty diner food.

And the woman who'd caught my eye? Well, she settled onto the counter stool right next to me, which got my hackles up. Women, as a rule, didn't just sit down at a diner counter next to men they didn't know. Especially men who looked like I did.

And anything out of the ordinary usually got my hackles up.

And this woman was anything but ordinary.

She was fucking beautiful. And most strikingly, she smelled like an angel.

She looked a little tired, probably from the bus ride, and was wearing a moderate case of bed head—sleeping on a bus will do that to you—but thick brown curls nevertheless spilled down her back. When she glanced at me, her green eyes—a little bloodshot—glittered like precious jewels in the dreariness of the truck stop surroundings.

A beautiful woman in the middle of a restaurant full of truck drivers.

You didn't see that every day.

"Bro, would you quit staring at that chick next to you?" Dutch whispered, elbowing me lightly. "We gotta eat and leave. Don't even think of chatting her up."

For Christ's sake. I was an operator, not a monk.

I tilted my head towards him and hissed, "Mind your own business, dude. I'll talk to her if I want."

I didn't even have to look at him to know he'd rolled his eyes at me. But he knew better than to try and cockblock me. I'd been in shittown for too long, and hadn't seen a beautiful woman in even longer. If all I could do was sit and smell this woman for a few minutes, I was damn well going to.

'Course I suppose *I* could have been cockblocking *him*. But hey, the woman had sat next to *me*, hadn't she?

Still, Dutch tried to distract me. "Christian, do we

need to get any more supplies before heading up the hill?"

"Huh? What?"

He took a deep breath, and tried again. "I said, do we need to get anything else before we go home? Supplies? Stuff like that?"

"Oh. Right. No, man, we're good. We got all the shit we need."

Well, we didn't have *everything* we needed. There weren't any women like the one next to me up on the mountain. Unfortunately, other than a few doe and maybe squirrels, the female population of Savage Mountain was severely lacking.

"Well, there is one thing we still need, now that I think of it," Dutch said.

God, I wished he'd just stop talking.

"What, Dutch? What do we need?" I asked impatiently.

"We still need a housekeeper. It's been months since the last one bailed and you know the four of us are shitty cleaners."

"Well, go put a notice on that bulletin board over there," I said, gesturing with my chin. "I'm sure someone'll pick it up."

He gave me a dirty look, and got up.

Finally, alone.

I took a quick glance at my neighbor. "You haven't touched anything on your plate," I said to her, grabbing the only opportunity I might have to talk to her where Dutch wasn't up my ass.

Her hands were balled into little fists, and she looked up in surprise, like she hadn't even realized I was there. "Oh. You're right," she said, shaking some gorgeous long hair out of her eyes.

She picked up her fork and pushed scrambled eggs around on her plate. She still didn't eat anything though, and deep inside a little part of me started to feel uneasy. I knew that faraway look her eyes wore, and it wasn't there because something nice had happened.

Something was off.

"Miss, I don't mean to be intrusive, but you look like… well, you look like something's not okay."

That was putting it mildly. She looked like she was about to go ballistic.

I guess I'd struck a nerve. Her back straightened and she looked around with wide eyes. Her fork fell out of her hand and tumbled to the ground with a loud clatter, causing her to jump.

She shook her head. Rubbing her temples, she nearly whimpered.

Okay, all was not well in this woman's world.

"Here, you can have my fork. I didn't use it, burgers are not fork food." I said, handing her mine while trying to keep it light.

She looked up at me gratefully, and warning lights

again went off in my head. How long had it been since someone had done something nice for her? Cripes.

And those eyes. Her gaze locked with mine, like she was desperately wanting to tell me something. I wasn't sure what, but my cock twitched *hello*, too.

Down boy. This was not the time for him to be interfering. I'd cockblock myself if I had to.

She looked back at her plate, and then back up at me, as if she were trying to screw up the courage to say something.

Taking a deep breath, she spoke tentatively. "Um, I hope you don't mind, but I overheard you and your friend talking. That you needed a housekeeper?"

"Oh. Yeah. You know someone? You can't be asking for yourself. What do you do?" I asked. She definitely did not look like someone who cleaned houses. Her hands were soft, and her nails, while short and neat, were painted a perfect red.

I pegged her for a—

"Nurse. I'm actually a nurse. But I'm interested in your housekeeper position," she said.

"What? Why?"

That sounded rude but I couldn't help myself. *She* wanted to clean *my* house?

Actually, that didn't sound half bad.

I could picture her running around in a little maid's costume, bending over to dust off my—

There was a tap on my shoulder.

"C'mon," Dutch said. "We gotta hit the road."

Of course. I gave him the stink eye as I slid off my stool. "I know, Dutch. But hey, this lovely lady right here is interested in our housekeeping position."

I pulled out some cash to cover both our bills, and laid it on the counter.

"My treat?"

Big player I was, spending a whopping ten bucks. Woo-hoo.

She smiled weakly, and looked at Dutch. "I over-heard you guys talking. Hope you don't mind. I'm um, looking for a new gig."

She forced a pathetic little smile, and I swear it nearly broke my heart.

Dutch, on the other hand, looked her up and down. "Really? You want to clean for us? You don't get paid much, pocket change really, but you do get free room and board, and our place is awesome."

Her eyes widened, and I swear her face lit up in a heart-stopping smile. "Oh, yes, I'll do it. That sounds great!"

Great? There was nothing great about cleaning up after four mountain men. In fact, I think you'd have to be an idiot to sign up for such a shit job, regardless of free room and board and nice views. When Dutch said pocket change, he wasn't lying. Like, enough to buy lunch at this diner once a week sort of money.

"Well, cool. I'll give you our number and we can set

up a time to talk next week." Dutch took a pen out of his pocket and began to scribble on a napkin.

She shook her head, frowning. "Oh, I can start right away."

"Don't you have to, you know, go home and pack or something?" I asked.

She looked to the end of the counter and then back to us. "Nope. Ready to go."

At this point, alarm bells were going off in my head. Time to find out what the hell was up. I stepped close to her and lowered my voice. "All right. What's your name?"

She looked up at me with those damnably beautiful green, pleading eyes. "Mari."

"Okay, Mari. I'm Christian. This is Dutch. Now that we've been introduced, I want to say it's clear that you've got some shit you're dealing with. Care to tell us what it is?"

She shook her head slowly. "I don't know what you mean."

Yeah, right.

I hardened my voice a little, not mean but stern. "You're nervous as hell, you keep looking towards the end of the counter, and you are ready to jump in a car with two strangers and go home with them. That isn't normal."

Her bottom lip shook. "Okay. Okay. See the guy at the end of the counter? The one with the backwards cap?"

The guy who kept looking over at us, with a pistol clearly stuffed down the back of his jeans? I'd been watching him since we'd walked the door. The motherfucker was clearly up to no good. "Yeah."

Mari swallowed. "He's trying to kill me."

2

____

MARI

OH, IF ONLY I'D STAYED HOME THAT NIGHT DOING something civilized like painting my toenails, folding laundry, watching *Survivor*, or giving myself a bikini wax. While watching *Survivor*.

But no, I'd agreed to go to the party from hell with my friend Luci, hosted by people who made the girls from *Jersey Shore* look like debutants.

Foul language and raised voices floated through the air toward me together with the smell of cigarettes and cheap beer. From the sound of it, a girl fight was brewing, and someone was already talking about taking off 'her hoops'.

In response, I heard someone spit. Never a good sign.

A voice shrilled, "I'll teach you to spit at me, you skanky crack-head!"

Cheers erupted. It was always good to have a posse behind you at times like that.

Being the nosy bitch I was, I strolled around the corner of the house to get a look at the uproar. In my everyday world, you didn't see women trying to take each other down. Not physically, anyway.

The sight that greeted me was a skinny, stringy-haired blonde lunging at a much beefier brunette, her face twisted into an ugly mask. "I'm gonna rip out those fake ass extensions, whore."

My money was on the bigger girl. But on the other hand, the skinny one was mad as hell. Mean looking, too.

"Just try it, bitch!" The brunette's hair was down to her waist, teased on top. She was pretty in a sort of dirty girl kind of way, with sharp, drawn-on eyebrows, black lip liner, and a tank top that looked like she'd cut the lower six inches off.

She flew at the blonde, and while I knew the wise move for me would have been to get the hell out of there, I was fascinated in a sick and probably unhealthy way. Like watching a bad car accident.

After a frantic half minute of rolling around in the dirt and weeds, the blonde jumped up in triumph, victoriously holding a fistful of long dark hair with little clips hanging off the ends.

She screamed proudly. "Ah, bitch, you got the Dollar General weave, you didn't even get them sewn in, you cheap-ass ho." The skinny one danced around while the brunette rubbed her raw scalp. Some of the crowd started joining in the chants like it was a sports event.

That was enough. I hightailed it out of there. I didn't want to be next.

I approached a group of guys observing the girl fight with disinterest.

"Hey, have you seen Luci anywhere?" I asked the dude I was pretty sure was her cousin. He was the one who'd invited us—well, invited Luci—promising he had a nice friend for her to meet.

Never mind that Luci and I were nurses, and that nurses met men all the time. I mean, we didn't want to date all of them, but we definitely had options. And those options usually had all their teeth. And spoke in full sentences.

"Oh." He turned, looking me up and down approvingly. "Marisa?"

"Um, no. It's Mari."

He looked at me like he couldn't give a shit, and that the only thing on his mind was my bra size.

"Yeah, right. Cool." He turned back to his buds, who were passing around a bottle of Jack.

"I was asking you where Luci was," I said, tapping him on the shoulder.

He turned slowly, wiping his mouth with the back of his hand.

"Why are you so worried about my cousin?" he asked, head tilted, his friends tittering behind him.

"I'm not. Never mind." I hurried the hell out of there.

It was the last time I was letting Luci take me to a party. I'd had enough of her cray-cray relatives and their white trash manners. I didn't care if her cousin had promised to introduce her to freaking Prince Harry.

To comfort myself, I grabbed myself a Bud out of a cooler full of melted ice since the keg had long since run dry, and wandered into the house looking for my friend. You'd think a nurse would have enough sense to stay away from a party full of low-lifes. But no, Luci was that girl everyone knew who never quite got over her high school thing for bad boys, the ones with no jobs, no prospects, but lots of priors. It was the nursing thing—the drive to take care of people.

Me, I was over it. I'd patch them up, but that stopped at the doors to the ER.

The house, with its dirty carpet and stained walls, was quiet since most of the party had spilled into the yard. But a sound coming from the top of the stairs grabbed me. I figured it was two partygoers getting it on, but then I heard a muffled 'no'.

I didn't like that. Not at all.

My stomach churned, and I leaned against the wall until the sick feeling passed.

I crept up the steps, listening to other strange noises like a body banging into things.

I just wanted to go home. Preferably with Luci.

Another muffled 'no,' and I knew who it was.

I followed the sounds to a hall closet, wishing I had my mini pepper spray. It wasn't much, but it was better than a half-full can of beer.

My heart beating wildly, I pulled the door open to find Luci pressed against a wall, some guy's arm across her neck, his other hand pulling her clothes off. In her drunken state, she couldn't fight him off, and with his arm cutting off her air, couldn't even scream.

I was pretty sure that was the guy she was to meet that night, thanks to her dirt-bag cousin.

"Luci!"

She looked at me, wild with fear, clawing so hard at the wall that her nails were broken and bleeding. There was a big gash on her knee, and one of her shoes was missing.

Seeing me, she got a burst of energy, and somehow wormed out from under the guy. But he moved faster, and knocked her to the ground where she sprawled, half in the closet and half in the hallway.

"Get off her!" I screamed, my voice trembling even as I froze in terror.

Undeterred, an ugliness crossed the guy's face that made my skin crawl.

"Shut up, bitch. Get the fuck out," he said, pointing at the door.

"Leave her alone," I said in my best fake badass voice. You learn to be pretty assertive as a nurse, but that doesn't prepare you for dealing with someone trying to hurt your best friend.

"I told you GET THE FUCK OUT," he bellowed, pulling Luci off the floor with one hand and waving at me with the other.

When I didn't budge, he took a step toward me, and something snapped inside. Before I could even think, I grabbed a dead houseplant with two brown stalks sticking out from the dirt, and swung it at him with all my might. Crashing into the side of his head, he was sent flying backwards, screaming.

A dead houseplant did all that?

"Luci, let's get out of here," I said, reaching for her.

But she stood still, just staring at the guy on the floor, who was on his side, facing away. Not moving.

"Oh, god," she moaned, pointing at him.

"Luci, c'mon. We have to get out of here."

I pulled her arm, but she kept looking at the guy and pointing, and when I took a closer look I knew why she'd screamed.

One of the dead stalks from the houseplant had stuck in his eye socket. Deep. Blood was everywhere. And he was motionless.

Had I killed him? With a freaking *houseplant*?

How is that even possible?

I felt his neck for a pulse. Not a damn thing.

Fuck.

"C'mon," I rasped, as I yanked Luci behind me. My car was close and if we didn't attract any attention, we could hit the road before anyone realized what had happened.

My heart was pounding and my stomach roiling. As a nurse, I saw gruesome things all the time, but I was not usually the cause of them.

Hustling past the guys doing shots of Jack, and the girls who were still screaming at each other, we escaped unnoticed. I stuffed Luci in the passenger seat and ran around to the driver's side. I had the car started and in *drive* before I'd even closed my door, that's how fast I was moving. I just wanted to get the hell out of there and call the cops. Fuck, I was going to be arrested. I just knew it. But I'd saved my friend.

I squealed down the street, shaking so hard my teeth were chattering.

"We gotta call the cops. Luci, get the phone out of my purse." I floored it to make a yellow light.

"No! You can't call the cops on those guys! They're in gangs. They're serious bad news. Some of their relatives are cops. They won't protect you," she said in a trembling voice.

Gangs? What the fuck? Now *I* wanted to kill her, too.

"You brought me to a party with *gang members?*" I yelled. "Are you fucking crazy? We are responsible, professional women. We can't be hanging with people like that."

Okay, maybe I shouldn't have pointed that out, but I was in the moment. Luci buried her head in her hands, and the sobs started. "I... I wanted to do my cousin a favor... and meet... his friend."

If Luci was going to be useless, I'd rummage for the phone myself.

"Are you fucking kidding me? That guy attacked you. You can't hang around with people like that. Ever. It doesn't matter what your cousin wants."

She nodded, sniffling, the overhead streetlights illuminating her blonde hair. Light, dark, light, dark, as we moved in and out of their glow.

Suddenly, her phone began to ring.

"Oh shit, it's my cousin!" she shrieked. "What should I do?"

"DON'T answer it Luci. Don't," I yelled.

I pressed harder on the accelerator, like that would make him go away. It would be a miracle if I didn't cause an accident.

3

MARI

In the ten minutes it took to reach Luci's house, her phone had not stopped ringing. Not for a moment, to the point I lost count of the number of times her crazy cousin had called. He'd hang up and just redial without leaving a message.

He didn't need to leave a message, though. We knew why he was calling.

The moment I dropped Luci at her apartment, I was going to call the cops. I didn't care if those guys were in gangs, it was the right thing to do. Sure, I'd be in trouble initially, but when I explained what had happened, they'd understand.

Right?

I mean, could you even arrest a person for killing via a houseplant? Wasn't that a clear-cut instance of self-defense?

Assault with a deadly houseplant.

When I pulled up, Luci opened her car door, looking around nervously. "I think we should keep quiet about this. Just pretend it never happened."

"Luci, a guy is dead," I said. "You don't just walk away from something like that. At least I don't. For Christ's sake, we're nurses, we're supposed to *save* people, not kill them."

She shook her head. "No, Mari. This is different. You don't know these people. I do. I grew up with them. Forget it ever happened."

I just looked at the steering wheel in front of me. This was insane… but she was completely serious.

"It's two a.m. I'm tired. Let's put our heads together first thing in the morning, okay?" I asked, buying some time to convince her to support me. If I reported anything without her to back me up, the situation could get even worse.

"Yeah. And Mari?"

"What?"

"You saved me. Thank you."

At least I'd done something right.

I'D NO SOONER GOTTEN home, still shaking, and still planning on calling the cops, when my cell rang.

"Luci, what's up?"

Her voice was shaking. "Y… you… gotta get out."

"Huh? What? I can barely understand you."

"I… I… oh my god, Mari… "

"Luci, you are making no sense. What is going on? I'm so tired. I want to go to bed. Are you okay?"

She took a deep inhale. "Y… yes. I'm okay. But you aren't. Get out."

Oh my god, this girl was killing me.

"What do you mean *get out?*"

"My cousin and his friends just came by my apartment. They forced me to tell them what happened."

"Okay. Well, they need to know their friend was attacking you."

"They're coming over your place. *Now.* You need to get out," she wailed.

"*My* house? How the hell do they know where I live?"

Oh.

Right. Thanks, Luci.

I hung up the phone and looked around my apartment in a panic. I had five, ten minutes tops.

Oh my god, I was running from a freaking gang.

I reached into the tampon box under my sink where I'd stashed my emergency piggy bank, a thousand or so dollars in cash. I stuffed it into my purse and looked wildly around my apartment. I pulled on some sneakers and grabbed a down puffer since I had no idea where I was going or what I was doing.

Going to my front door, I locked the deadbolt, as if that would stop a bunch of thugs, and ran down the stairs to the back of my apartment building where we put the trash. Sneaking into the dank and smelly alley, I inched to the corner where I could see my car. The coast looked clear, at least at the moment.

Gathering my courage, I sprinted to my car, and left the parking lot by the back way.

But what the hell was I supposed to do next?

I DROVE straight to the police station. They'd help me. Even if I had to explain things three times over, they'd resolve the nightmare the evening had turned into. So what if the gang guys had family in the police. They had to help me. Right?

I pulled into the station's empty lot. When I got to the door, I pressed the buzzer and was permitted into a lobby where a lone female cop sat behind a bulletproof glass wall. Seemed like a good place to be safe.

"May I help you ma'am?" she asked, yawning.

Just then my phone buzzed with a text.

don't go to the cops. it will just make things worse

Well, fuck.

"I'm sorry, I need to make a call. I'll be right back," I said to the woman at the desk.

I stepped outside.

"Luci, what the fuck do you mean don't get the cops involved? I could end up dead at the hands of those guys," I hissed.

"Don't Mari. Just don't. The cops can't help you now."

"Well, what the hell am I supposed to do? Go home and let them do whatever gang people do to people they're mad at?"

"Listen to me, Mari. You need to get out of town—"

"*What?*"

"Go to the Greyhound station and get on a bus. Leave your car behind. They know it and will find you."

"You have *got* to be kidding—"

"Go *now*," Luci said, her voice breaking slightly. "These guys have a big network and have all sorts of people in their pockets. Keep your head down. I'll let you know when you can come back."

With one last glance at the police station lobby, against every bit of better judgment I'd ever had in my entire life, I got back in my car.

"Okay," I said, my voice flat and defeated. I couldn't believe I was running. I'd done nothing but save my friend.

"Thank you, Mari. You'll be okay," Luci said, her voice full of false hope. "I just need some time, and until I figure out what to do, you can't be around. These guys take action first, and ask questions later."

I looked up the Greyhound station on my phone's map. I knew I'd driven by it a time or two, but when I saw the address, I nearly freaked. It was close to the part of town we'd just fled from… but it seemed like the best option at the moment. Maybe the only option

"Luci, where do I go? I'm scared."

"I know, Mari. Just get on the first bus out of town, and we'll figure it out from there."

"Cover for me at work, okay? Make something up."

"Of course I will. Don't worry about that. I'll tell them you have a sick relative you have to take care of. Something like that. Just go."

***

"WHAT CAN I help you with, Miss?" asked the perky woman selling Greyhound tickets.

"Um," I replied, looking at the old fashioned board behind her. "I need a ticket. Somewhere."

Her expression never wavered. I imagined she'd heard it all. I mean, isn't the bus station where people go who really wanted to disappear?

"Where do ya want a ticket to, honey? We service nearly four thousand destinations in North America and have approximately thirty thousand buses on the road every day."

She smiled broadly, like she was in a T.V. commercial.

Well, shit.

I took a deep breath and smiled. It wouldn't do to let on my desperation. I leaned closer to mirror her friendliness.

"It looks like on the schedule up there, the next bus leaves in one hour."

"It sure does," she chirped, happy as ever. "Although, see that bus right there? Pulling out of the lot?" she asked, pointing out the door at a bus backing up.

"Yes! Can I get on that one? Can you stop it?"

She smiled serenely. "No. We can't stop it. I just wanted you to know that that was the next one that was actually leaving."

Gee thanks, lady.

"Okay, then I'll take the bus after that one."

"Super!" she said. "That's thirty dollars. And may I see your ID?"

Shit.

"Do you have to see my ID?" Time to lay it on. I leaned closer to her and lowered my voice. Even though no one was around. "I'm, um, trying to get away from a dangerous situation."

Her eyes opened wide. "Oh my gosh, honey. That's terrible. I'll tell you what. Just put whatever name you want to use down here on this piece of paper, and that's what I'll enter in the system."

"Thank you. Thank you so much." I gave her my thirty dollars and wrote a name on the piece of paper: *Martha Washington.*

———

I settled into a plastic chair, and began reading on my phone. The waiting room wasn't as dirty as I'd thought it would be, and the seats were actually decent —plastic but curved to fit my butt. Just as I was opening my latest thriller novel, my phone buzzed. It was Luci.

they're on their way

What the fuck? My thumbs flew on the screen, typing back furiously.

what are u talking about? u said I'd be safe at the bus station

Great. Just great. I stood, looking frantically for the restrooms. The ticket clerk had gone back to her *Reader's Digest*, paying no attention to me. I ran to the ladies' room, into the last stall, and locked the door behind me.

They wouldn't find me here, would they? I looked at my watch.

Forty-two minutes to go.

Cripes, was I a dumbass. The ladies' room was the first place they'd look. At least that's what happened in the movies.

I left the bathroom, and approached the clerk again. "Do you think I could rest behind your counter while I'm waiting for the bus? I'd feel safer there."

Her previously sweet disposition slid off her face

like ice cream on a hot day. Maybe she'd messed up her crossword puzzle?

She looked around the empty station. "No. No you may not come behind this counter. That's a violation of company policies."

"Well, so was your taking my fake name—"

Her eyes widened and she gasped. Now I'd done it.

She shook a finger in my face. "Now you look here, missy. I don't want any of your trouble. I know your type, and it follows you everywhere you go."

Had someone just slapped me across the face? Because it sure felt like it.

I was a *type*?

And trouble *followed me*?

"Excuse me. I am a nurse. I save lives—"

"Please have a seat in the waiting area, miss, or I will have to call the police."

Part of me wanted to say *go ahead, I'll happily sit here while you do that*, but I didn't. Instead I looked down, nodding. Satisfied she'd put me in my place, she returned to whatever *Reader's Digest* serial was riveting her.

I headed back toward the rest rooms, forming a better idea. I hoped.

At the men's room door, I glanced back to make sure the clerk wasn't watching, and scooted inside, running for the graffiti covered stall next to two filthy urinals. It wasn't the perfect solution, but would they think to look for me in a men's room?

I sat on top of the toilet seat, the stench of unflushed urine burning my nose. With fifteen minutes until departure, I heard the sound of people arriving in the waiting room. Guess I wouldn't be the only nutjob getting on a bus at four a.m.

I shot Luci a text.

bus leaving soon. haven't seen anyone looking for me

She didn't reply.

She probably went to bed, all safe and sound, while her best friend's life was in danger, I told myself bitterly. How is it that I saved her, but I ended up with the shit end of the stick?

A familiar but garbled perky voice—yes, it was my friend from the front counter—was making an announcement. Five minutes.

I looked at the time on my phone and made my plan. In three minutes, which would give me two minutes to spare, I was going to walk quickly from the men's room to the bus with the hope that if there were someone following me, they'd not be able to catch me.

In the meantime, a couple guys came in and out of the men's room. The urinals flushed, they washed their hands, and they left. No one had needed the stall, fortunately.

So far so good.

At the sixty second countdown, I started taking deep breaths. It wouldn't do to freak out.

Three...

Two...

One…

I slipped out of the stall and silently opened the men's room door an inch. There were a few people milling around the waiting area, saying goodbye to friends, grabbing their bags. Things like that. From where I stood, I could see the bus. I yanked the door open, hurried across the waiting room and out the door on the other side, and dashed up the steps to the bus.

The driver greeted me with a nod, taking my ticket without even looking at me. I moved to the back of the half-empty bus in order to have a view of it, and settled in for a long drive.

Just before the bus took off, one last man boarded. I wouldn't even have noticed, except that he walked down the entire aisle, and took the seat next to me.

I was dead.

No doubt about it.

4

____

MARI

THREE HOURS INTO THE TRIP, WHEN THE GREYHOUND had reached our first rest stop, I'd parked my butt next to a couple beefy guys sitting at the counter of a truck stop diner, thinking desperately of a way to engage them and maybe ask for their help.

Two very *hot* beefy guys.

I may have been about to die, but I wasn't dead yet, for heaven's sake.

The one furthest from me looked like a damn NFL player—I mean, I had to crane my neck to look up at him from where I was sitting. The other, nearly as tall and wide, looked like he'd walked out of the pages of

GQ with his salt and pepper hair and piercing blue eyes.

The two stood out even more because everyone else in the truck stop diner looked like a—well, a trucker, with the exception of the sad group of people that had just gotten off my bus for a fifteen-minute break. And then there was the gangbanger waiting for a chance to kill me. He'd sat his ass at the end of the counter and pulled a ball cap low on his brow.

I didn't have much time, so gave them the short version of my story.

"Okay," said the one who'd introduced himself as Christian. "Someone's trying to *kill* you?"

He looked both puzzled and suspicious and glanced over at his friend, Dutch, who was obviously skeptical too about what I was saying.

I had to think fast. These guys were just trying to get home. If I wanted to be on their train, I had to convince them to let me on.

Otherwise, death was imminent. *My* death.

I gestured with a slight tilt of the head. "He's following me," I said quickly. "And he's going to kill me. Please take me with you. Please. He's in a gang, and one of his buddies tried to rape my friend. I knocked the guy out with a houseplant, and now they're after me."

I looked between their faces, covered with a mix of confusion and surprise.

"You knocked someone out? Why would they be after you for that?" Dutch asked.

I took a deep breath. "I think… I might have killed him."

They looked at each other again, and Christian leaned in, keeping his voice low and professional.

"You *think* you killed him? Or you *did* kill him?"

I resisted rolling my eyes. "Does it matter? He's after me. I could use some help."

Christian rubbed the scruff on his chin. "I don't know…" he said slowly.

They stood there, looking at me, trying to assess whether I was worth their trouble.

"Please," I begged, looking from one to the other.

Christian sighed. "Do you have any stuff?"

"Nope. Just my bag here, and the clothes on my back," I said, patting my pocket. "And my GTFO money."

Jackpot. I didn't care if I had to scrub the tile on their bathroom with my personal toothbrush, I'd do anything these guys asked.

Yes, *anything*.

What girl would turn *that* down? But, first things first.

"Listen," Christian said to his friend. "I'll take her. You pick a fight with the guy so we can get out before he follows us. We'll be ready for you in the Jeep as soon as you've laid him out."

I grabbed the buttermilk biscuit off my plate and stuffed it in my bag. I'd not eaten a bite, and who knew when I'd have the chance to again.

"Roger that," Dutch said as Christian and I slowly moved toward the door.

Dutch strolled down to the end of the counter like he was headed for the men's room. When he neared the guy who was after me, he shoulder-chucked him just hard enough to knock him off his seat.

"Hey," the guy yelled, his coffee flying as he tumbled to the floor. Amid a litany of swearing, he scrambled for the cap that rolled just out of his reach, revealing the ink on his head. Gangster for sure.

"You fucker, I'll—"

His threats quickly turned into screams as his fingers were stepped on by my new oversized friend.

The hubbub had attracted the attention of the truckers—to some extent. The ones next to him at the counter moved their plates out of the way, while others stopped their conversation and set down their coffee to see what the fuss was about. When no guns came out, they casually returned to what they'd been doing before, shaking their heads and chuckling.

Maybe fights broke out all the time in truck stops? Whatever. I didn't plan to stick around long enough to find out. But I had to say, the way my new friend took care of business gave me the kind of lift I didn't think I'd ever feel again.

Maybe I wasn't going to die that day.

Maybe.

"C'mon," Christian said, pulling me out the door by the hand.

Dutch nodded at us while keeping the guy pinned to the floor, and I reluctantly began to run. I wouldn't have minded seeing him finished off, but I reminded myself my top priority was to get the hell out of Dodge.

"Where's the money you owe me, asshole?" Dutch bellowed at the guy for the benefit of the entire room.

Oh. I *got* it. Create a plausible reason to smack the hell out of the guy, one that the truckers might believe while not noticing me slip out the door. But how would we keep the guy from following us or seeing our license plate?

"What's going on? What's Dutch doing in there?" I asked as we headed for Christian's Jeep.

He glanced over his shoulder to assess the fight's progress. "He'll be out in a sec. He has to rough the guy up enough to keep him from following us."

My bus was boarding again, the driver having closed up the luggage compartment underneath. I watched the last passenger get on and remembered the paperback I'd left. "My book—"

"You wanna go with them or something?" Christian asked, gesturing with his chin.

"No!" I jumped into the Jeep and turned to see what I could from the backseat. A book over my life?

Nah.

Not a minute later, Dutch came bounding out the door, leaving my pursuer writhing on the floor. I wasn't sure what he'd done, but I was pretty sure it involved inflicting pain.

Cripes, these guys were badasses. I'd hitched my car to the right train it seemed, at least at the moment.

"Hit it Christian," Dutch said, jumping in, slamming the car door and setting a gun on the dashboard.

Wait. Was that his gun? Or the gang guy's gun?

Either way, there was now a freaking gun in the car.

Christian jammed the Jeep into *reverse* and we screeched backward, then peeled out of the truck stop parking lot and onto the empty freeway.

Out the back window I lost sight of the guy on the floor of the diner. All I could see, getting smaller and smaller, were the headlights of the Greyhound bus as it pulled onto the road and headed in the opposite direction.

The smell of the truck stop and thoughts of the guy trying to annihilate me faded as Christian drove, concentrating and ensuring the needle on the Jeep never strayed more than five miles over the speed limit.

"All right, Mari," Dutch said, twisting his hulking body around to address me. "What's the story with your being followed? I'd like to hear the whole thing."

I didn't blame him. He had just assaulted a guy purely on my say-so.

"Like I said, I'm a nurse. A co-worker, also my best friend, invited me to a party at her cousin's. She's from a hard part of town, and her cousins are not the nicest of people, but I went because she begged me. I was looking for her at the end of the night to head home, and found her in a room with some guy who was choking her, I think trying to rape her. She was too drunk to defend herself. So... I hit him with a potted plant."

Even though it was dark in the car, I could see in the passing glow of streetlights that Dutch was missing a piece of his ear. That, coupled with the way he took down the guy in the diner, had me wondering who the hell *he* was, just like they were probably wondering who the hell *I* was.

Who the hell were *either* of them? And what the hell was I getting into?

Bit late for that.

"And you think you killed him?" Christian asked. "I mean, you're a nurse. Wouldn't you know?"

"Yeah. Pretty sure I did," I said in a small voice. "I checked for a pulse, but I was freaked, and I might have messed up. We hauled ass instead. Either way, my girl-friend called me after I dropped her off to say the guys were coming to get me. I took off for the bus station and thought I'd gotten away until this guy planted himself next to me on the bus. When we stopped for our break, I ran inside as fast as I could, thinking he couldn't do anything with a lot of people around."

"Well," Dutch said after I'd finished, "you're lucky you latched onto us. You might have been dead before the bus reached its next destination."

That last comment hit me harder than anything had in the last six hours. He was right...

"Pull over, please. I think I'm going to be sick."

Christian maneuvered the Jeep to the side of the highway just in time for me to lean my head out and lose what little was in my stomach. I might have been with a couple of the world's best protectors, but the abject fear I'd experienced over the last several hours just culminated in a big *fuck you* from my body.

As we got back on the road, I pulled out my cell to let Luci know I was okay.

No signal. Great. Guess I was in one of those dead zones.

"So what about you guys?" I asked.

Silence greeted me, and the guys glanced at each other quickly.

Okayyy…

"We have a place on Savage Mountain. Nice place, remote and private, quiet and peaceful," Christian said.

"How many of you are living there?" I asked.

"Four."

Christ, this was like pulling teeth. I leaned forward, onto their seat, to see if I could better engage them.

"What do you do for a living? How do you get by up there?"

Dutch answered after another glance, his voice no nonsense and flat. "We're pretty much retired."

"Oh." Retired? What, did they win the lottery or something? "Well, that's nice. Retired from what?"

This time Dutch turned to face me. "We're retired from the military. We lead simple but satisfying lives."

Then he turned back around, like that answered everything.

Okay. Guess that was the end of that line of questioning. Still, it didn't make sense. I mean, the guys weren't old enough to be twenty-year retired military, and neither seemed the kind to be 'medically retired' either. So… what the hell?

I allowed myself one more question. I didn't want to risk getting kicked out, especially since I had no idea where we were, or what the hell Savage Mountain was.

"Hey guys?" I asked.

"Yeah?"

"Um, do you think we'll pass a place with some food? I didn't eat back there at the truck stop, and am kind of starving."

"We can't stop," Christian said, a lot more warmly than Dutch was. "Too risky. You'll have to wait until we arrive at the cabin. Sorry. We have food at the house and you can eat when we get there."

Eh. I'd survive. I lay down on the Jeep's backseat, bunching up my purse to use as a pillow. Before I did, however, I dug the biscuit out that I'd swiped off my breakfast plate and sunk my teeth into the soft, buttery dough. It was comforting in a discomforting way. I mean, how could something be so delicious and pleasing when everything had just been pulled out from under me?

I thanked my lucky stars these guys had crossed my

path, and fingers crossed, they'd feel just as grateful that I'd stumbled into theirs. Even if just for the short term.

5

MARI

WHEN I OPENED MY EYES, A REDDISH SUNSET STREAMED through the Jeep's windows, leaving me hot and sweaty. Before I could push myself up from my prone position to see anything, we hit a bump so hard I bounced off the backseat and rolled to the floor.

"My god. What was that?" I asked, pulling myself back up.

"Hey, you're awake," Christian said, looking at me in the rear-view mirror with those insane baby blues. "You've been out a little over an hour. Perfect timing."

Running for your life will do that.

Dutch twisted toward me, his broad shoulders barely fitting in the passenger seat. "The last few miles to the cabin are on dirt roads. We've got some pretty big potholes up here, so hang on and try to get comfortable. I'll slow down some, but it won't be smooth, to be honest."

Um, yeah, no kidding. I noticed he had a strong grip on the 'oh shit' handle just next to his head and figured I better do the same.

When I got my ass under me, I saw we were surrounded by trees and more trees on both sides of the Jeep. Then there was dirt road behind us, and dirt road ahead of us.

That was it. Trees and dirt road.

Perhaps I had made a mistake?

Yes, I'd been scared to death at the truck stop. But to go off with a couple mountain men, I mean complete and total strangers, was the act of an idiot. Right?

What the fuck had I done? What if these guys were bigger psychos than the ones I was running from?

I should have just called the cops when the whole thing started. Not listened to Luci.

Shit, if I'd not listened to Luci I'd never gone to that fucking party.

So many mistakes. So little time.

After bouncing around the backseat for another hour despite my death grip on the seat in front of me, the road opened to a clearing, and as we drove a little further, a massive house came into view. It was beautiful—a rustic mansion really, like something a billionaire would build as their mountain getaway.

Maybe this gig wouldn't be too bad after all. I was

totally up for a mini-vacation. On the other hand, if I were stuck with cleaning that entire place, I was screwed. Hello, Cinderella. I'd never see the light of day.

"We're here. Cool," I said, opening my car door the moment we stopped. I was dying to stretch my legs. And pee.

"Hey, hold on Mari. Could you please get back in the car?" Dutch asked.

"Oh. Sure." I pulled the door mostly closed. He looked at me hard, and I slammed it all the way. "What's up?"

"We need to talk to the other guys before we introduce you," he said. He walked up to the house, with Christian leading the way.

"Why?" I asked, but they were already gone.

Shit. They'd taken the keys, and the windows in the back seat were rolled up. So, I scrambled over the console into the front passenger seat to get some air. I crouched down low, not really sure why, straining to hear them speaking to another guy on the front porch.

I couldn't make out much, but what I did gather didn't make me feel better about my decision to come to Savage Mountain.

"I know dude, but she's hot as hell. You should see the tits on her…"

Oh. So that's how it was. What assholes. I fumed in my silence, with half a mind to tell their tacky asses off. But I needed them a lot more than they needed me.

So I kept my trap shut.

"…she's a fucking nurse, man…"

"…well, at least we have some help around the house for a bit…"

Voices rose and fell, and I caught something more about housekeeping and 'extra work,' whatever the hell that was. I strained to hear more, and while I did, I let the door to the glove box drop open.

Shit.

There, before me, was the gun Dutch had put on the dash after roughing up the dirtbag at the truck stop. In addition to it was *another* gun, and a badass-looking knife in a leather sheath. Did every mountain man have a stash of weapons? I mean, was this going to be an everyday thing?

Could you please pick up your gun so I can vacuum under it?

I could see it now.

And were they assuming nookie, under the 'extra work' category, was part of the bargain? Because if they did, they had another thing coming.

I looked up to see Dutch heading back over, and knew what I'd be dreaming about that night when I was alone. I grabbed one of the guns and the knife, and dropped them into the bottom of my purse, hoping I didn't end up shooting myself or anyone else. At the last second, I closed the glove box with my knee, just as Dutch waved me in.

"Hey, Mari, we're ready for you now. Just had to

talk to the guys about how you came to join us. We usually do a bit of vetting before bringing up a new person, but everyone's willing to let you stay on a trial basis."

Gee, thanks.

"What are you doing there in the front seat?" he asked, his brow furrowed.

"Oh, it was getting hot in the back and I couldn't open the window. I thought to get out of the car for some air, but I knew you didn't want me to." I pinched my purse closed so he couldn't see my contraband.

"Okay. Let's go, then."

He started back toward the house, but I caught his arm. "Hey, I have something I really need to say."

"What's that?" he asked, turning to face me.

"I heard you guys talking about me and I don't want anyone getting any funny ideas. 'Extra work' will not be done on my knees, understand?"

He bit his lip to keep from laughing, which *really* pissed me off. "Fair enough. Sorry about that. Sometimes we forget how to behave, we've been up here for so long."

"Thank you for the apology. Now, I'd like to return to… I don't know, wherever the closest town is."

He looked at me curiously. "Why?"

"I think you guys have gotten the wrong idea about me," I said.

Would that really be so bad…?

"Well, I think you've gotten the wrong idea about

us. But we can take you back down the mountain, no problem," he said.

"Okay, then. Super. I appreciate it." I turned to head back to the Jeep, hoping that wherever I ended up had a vacant hotel room.

"Mari?" he called after me.

"Yeah?" I asked, turning.

Goddamn, he was a sight to behold with about the strongest shoulders I'd ever seen on a man. Talk about cutting off your nose to spite your face—was it too late to reconsider leaving?

"We don't go back down until next week at the earliest."

I felt the blood drain from my face, and I clenched my fists.

Easy girl. Don't say something you'll regret. I clutched my purse closer, feeling the gun through the soft leather. I had no idea how to shoot, but my new weapons were strangely comforting.

He tilted his head at me. "C'mon. At least look at the place before you make up your mind about anything. Besides, you were right. We'll try to be on our best behavior. Deal?"

I said nothing, and just followed him.

In spite of my misgivings, I had to admit the house was freaking amazing. Yeah, the guys had called it a cabin, but it was so much more than that—kind of a cross between a mansion and a luxury hunting lodge.

But it was huge, an easy five thousand square feet. No fucking way I was cleaning that whole thing.

Footsteps crossed the house's front porch.

"Jesus, Christian, put some fucking clothes on," Dutch said. "Lady, remember?"

When I peered around his massive shape, Christian crossed our path, pulling a towel off his shoulders to cover his privates, but not until after I got a nice glimpse of them. He could walk around naked all the time as far as I was concerned.

"Sorry. Going for a swim," he said. "Feel free to join me," he called over his shoulder, the muscles of his naked, taut ass flexing with every step he took.

That was what Luci would call a *fine piece of meat*. A swim with him might have been pretty darn nice.

Dutch looked part amused, part annoyed. "Like I said, we're not used to women around here. It's been awhile."

I walked faster to keep up with him, tearing my eyes from Christian's naked backside getting smaller in the distance.

"What happened to the last person cleaning for you?" I asked.

"She was with us a year or so, but left to go travel in South America or some place like that. So, we're glad you're here," he said, holding the door to the house open for me.

Um, okay. I looked around the entrance hall. Jeez,

oak floors, good looking workmanship, recessed LED lighting… these guys were not exactly roughing it.

What the hell had I stumbled into? The Playboy mansion of the mountains?

A giant vaulted ceiling skyrocketed a good twenty feet into the air, and was hung with a chandelier made of some sort of antlers. One wall was all stone, with a massive fireplace in the middle. Another was floor-to-ceiling glass and overlooked a canyon. Opposite, through a big double doorway, was a gigantic open plan kitchen.

I let out a breath, shaking my head. "Dutch, I don't think I'll be able to clean this place for you. Maybe it was a mistake coming up here, you need a team at least."

He laughed. "Don't worry. We'll figure it out."

The sofas and chairs in the main room were clustered in cozy and intimate seating areas, sort of like a hotel lobby, and heavy oriental rugs covered large sections of the hardwood floor. Every surface was covered with expensive treasures.

Dutch must have noticed my mouth hanging open because he laughed.

"Yeah, it's an awesome place," he said, looking around in appreciation. "We're lucky to have it. Hey, how 'bout I show you to your room?"

He put his hand on the small of my back and pointed toward a huge spiral staircase.

"Where is all this from? It's just amazing," I said, doing a three sixty-degree-turn to take it all in.

"We've worked all over the world and collected things in our travels. C'mon," he said evasively, taking me by the hand.

At his touch, electricity fired through me. Gruff or not in the Jeep, I felt sheltered by him, protected, and turned on as hell. Following his massive form up the stairs, I watched him duck in order to avoid bumping his head.

"Here you go," he said, when we reached the end of a long hallway. "You're down here by yourself, with your own bathroom, so you have privacy. We guys are at the other end of the hall."

"Oh my god," I said, entering a room done in all white, with a four poster bed, a dressing table, and two comfy-looking reading chairs. This wasn't a log cabin room, this was a suite in a hotel. A *five star* hotel.

Something didn't add up.

I put my hands on my hips and looked hard at Dutch. "Okay. You guys aren't just retired military. Since when does a cleaning lady live in digs like this?"

He shrugged. "It's a nice house. What can I say? You good with this room?"

I spun around, feeling like a freaking princess. "Are you kidding? This is any woman's dream come true. I love it!"

He laughed, grinning. "Thought you might. Hey, you've had a long night. Feel like getting in a hot tub?"

Oh my god.

I tried to play it cool, but my effort was wasted.

I jumped up and down like a little kid. "*Now* you're talking. Lead the way." I had no bathing suit but it wouldn't be the first time I'd used my underwear as a close substitute.

I might have some cleaning to do for four strange mountain men, but it was going to be the most luxurious maid gig anyone had ever had.

6

Dutch

I WAS PRETTY SURE THE LOVELY MARI HAD NO FUCKING idea how to clean house, but I was all right with that. Of course, the other guys were going to be pissed at Christian and me for bringing her up to the cabin without clearing it first, but they'd get over it. Besides, like any of them would turn her away, anyway.

Men didn't turn away women like Mari. Ever. She was fucking stunning with that long dark hair, huge green eyes, and flawless skin. Too beautiful, too pure, too girl-next-door to deny.

It didn't hurt that I personally was a sucker for a woman in danger.

And yes, her tits were not to be believed.

I mean, could the guys blame me for thinking with my little head? It was bound to happen when you lived like we did. Besides, there was no harm in having a nurse around—someone to perform basic first aid when needed.

I knew the moment she saw the house, she'd be sold.

"So where's the hot tub?" she asked.

"Out on the deck out here," I said, opening the French doors to an overlook extending for miles. It was my favorite view on Savage Mountain, and one I enjoyed as often as possible.

Mari stood there taking it all in, when she turned to me.

"What are you guys doing up here? I mean you're in the middle of nowhere, but this house is palatial. And fancy. Look at this view," she said in awe.

Questions. There were always questions. And she was sniffing in the wrong direction.

"You don't need to know why we're here," I said, firmly but not unkindly. "Just accept that we are, and that you get to benefit from it."

She frowned at me, not buying it. I couldn't blame her. I'd be suspicious too. But the less she knew, the better for all of us.

"What is that noise?" she demanded, looking around in alarm as a sharp noise came from the other side of the house.

Was she just going to ask questions all day long? Christ, maybe bringing her to the cabin had been a mistake after all.

"One of the guys is at target practice. Remember, we're former military." I decided to leave it at that.

But not Mari.

"Can you teach me some time?" she asked, biting her lip. "I've always wanted to learn… if there's time?"

Those big eyes just about killed me, and she was so earnest, even if she didn't seem like the 'shooting type'. But after what someone like she had just been through, it was amazing what you'd be willing to do to survive. I knew that first-hand.

"Yeah, sure. You've never fired a weapon?" I asked her.

She rolled her eyes. "I'm a nurse. We don't use guns. We use needles."

She playfully slapped my arm, the first time we'd touched. I wanted to ask her to do it again, she felt so nice, but I didn't want to come off as a fucking loser, so I kept my mouth shut.

"Just look at this," she said when she saw the hot tub built into the side of the deck.

My favorite part of the house, it extended over the side of the mountain like a small infinity pool. It made living in the middle of nowhere with three dudes worthwhile.

"Isn't it insane?" I said, pulling my T-shirt off over my head. "I'm pretty much the only one who ever uses it unless someone's got a sore muscle or something."

I'd normally jump in the tub in my birthday suit, but figured I'd keep my skivvies on so she wouldn't run away screaming. Although if she were getting in butt-naked...

"I don't have a bathing suit," she said, as I flipped the switch to get things rolling in the tub. "Gonna use my undies, hope you don't mind."

Crap. "Yeah, figured you didn't. Underwear is fine, obviously. Or, you can take your clothes off and I'll look away. I can't see you underwater with the jets going. Or, you can take your clothes off and I'll watch. That's the one I'd vote for."

Fuck, I'd *pay* to see her unclothed, that's how jazzed I was to be getting in the hot tub with a gorgeous woman.

"Very funny. Turn around."

Her sneakers and jeans hit the deck, and she jumped in with a small *splash*. "I kept my underwear on, sorry to disappoint."

"It's all good," I said, settling into the steaming water. I leaned my head against the back of the tub and watched a hawk soar over the treetops below.

I didn't have the heart to tell Mari that the last housekeeper we had did such a shitty job cleaning we finally let her go. But the part about her going to South America wasn't a lie. Despite the low pay we offered, we'd given her a chunk of money so she'd stay quiet about our lifestyle. She'd be able to travel for years on it. Maybe never even work again if she lived carefully.

That's what I called a good deal.

And just like the last girl, Mari didn't look like the

most promising housekeeper in the world. Maybe we'd end up in the same situation as last time, but I hoped we'd have some fun along the way.

Actually, I was hoping to have some fun right away, if the pretty girl were into it. What I had in mind would be perfect for releasing a little of the stress she'd been under.

"You know, you're very beautiful, Mari," I said, my hand drifting under the water to grasp her fingers.

I took it as a good sign that she leaned her head against the tub and closed her eyes, her fingers wrapping around mine.

"Thank you," she said softly. "And thank you for getting rid of that guy and bringing me up here. You saved my life. And now, *this*. It's so incredibly relaxing. You're lucky to have this tub with this insane view." She sighed sweetly.

And now my dick was getting hard.

So I decided to test my luck.

I gently dragged a wet finger across her lips and down her neck. She smiled lightly.

Pushing my luck, I moved in front of her and put my hands on either side of her face, smoothing back the wet hair clinging to her cheeks. I passed my palm over her soft skin, and she turned, surprising me by pressing her lips into it. That was about all I could take.

And it was all the encouragement I needed.

I leaned into her just until our lips touched. I knew to take it slow with a girl like her, if for no other reason than she'd just been running for her life and was raw as hell.

But I was more than happy to do my duty and help her forget her troubles. It was the least I could do.

My hands wandered down to her bra straps, easing them carefully off her shoulders. I reached behind her to unhook the garment, and threw it up on the deck as her tits sprang free. Even in the water, they were heavy in my hands, perfect teardrops that filled each palm. I ran my thumbs over her stiff nipples and she kissed me back, her hunger evident.

My hands wandered further south, past her small waist to where her hips flared. There, I hooked my thumbs in her panties, and eased them down and below her bottom, where she sat on the tub's underwater bench.

I threw those onto the deck, as well.

"Mari-"

"I know... don't worry," she whispered. "Help me forget."

Her hands pressed against my chest and smoothed up my shoulders, where they rested behind my head. I planted small kisses down the side of her neck, slowly turning her so her back was to me. Reading my desire, she positioned herself to kneel on the tub's seat and laid her head down to rest on the ledge. Her breasts bobbed heavy in the water, and she moaned as I ran my hands over the cheeks of her bare ass.

"You like?"

"Yes… more please," she whispered happily. "Much more."

Fucking A. This beauty's behind, partially submerged in the water, was inches from my face, and I was more than happy to oblige. I dragged my fingers through her swollen lips, now soaked and slippery with excitement. In response, she pushed her ass back toward me.

I notched my forefinger at her pussy opening, and spread around her slick juice. God I was dying to bury my stiff dick in there, but that could come later, if she wanted it. For now, we'd just play.

I positioned another finger at her opening, and slowly pushed the two inside her, penetrating her inch by inch until she tensed, and I knew to pause. Her walls grasped me as I pulled back out, leaving her empty and wanting.

"Mmmm," she murmured. "Don't stop."

I put my lips to her ear. "You like that, beautiful? You like my rough fingers in your pussy?"

Her eyes fluttered open and she turned her head to smile at me. "Yeah," she said softly.

She was so fucking beautiful, naked and dripping wet. I almost exploded right there.

But I drove in again, as deeply as I could, and then drew back out, speeding up until I was pounding her pussy so hard she was holding on to the tub for purchase. Her thighs and tits made waves in the water, sloshing back and forth and all over the deck.

Who knew the girl was going to like it so rough?

"Ohhhh... I'm cominggg..." she moaned suddenly, pushing back hard against me.

Her head arched back and she cried out, her pussy squeezing against my hand for more, until she collapsed forward. I slipped my fingers out of her, patted her bottom, and got out of the tub. "Good girl. Very good girl."

She nodded, smiling happily, and I left her there as she watched me walk away.

She had a few lessons to learn, and they were starting now.

"Look, asshole. You either have a good hand or you don't," Victor said later that afternoon. He always wanted to go faster—his idea of good poker would have us playing a hundred hands in a night.

But Red wasn't to be rushed.

"Shut up. I'm thinking," he said.

"What's there to think about? Make a damn decision."

Christian and I looked at each other, amused. Every card game we played went down like this.

"Dude, you were a dick when we were in the Special Forces, and you're still a dick now. It's a miracle you got out alive," Victor said.

"Well, it's no thanks to you, buddy. I got shot five times because of your lame ass," Red retorted.

"How long are you going to keep blaming me for that?" Victor asked, rolling his eyes. "I was the one kept hostage. And it's not like you got shot anywhere important."

Everyone knew Victor was not to blame for any injuries Red sustained, but they still loved playing their game all the same.

"Can you two bitches shut up and keep playing? I'm tired of hearing you flap your gums," I said.

"Hey, watch what you're saying," Christian said, gesturing toward the door.

Mari stood there, wearing the leggings and tank top our last housekeeper had left behind. Her hair was freshly washed and dried, and without a stitch of makeup on her face, she was beyond stunning.

The guys glanced over her way, and then went right back to their cards.

I did the same thing. It wouldn't do to show her favor, as much as I'd been totally into the fun little session we'd had earlier.

"Hi guys," she said, sauntering into our game.

"Hey."

"Hi."

"What's up?"

Silence.

Yeah, we were pretty much ignoring her. And I felt a little bad about that. But our evening card game was just for us. She wasn't one of the guys. She'd learn that soon enough. I didn't like dissing her, but it had to be done. It was the way we did things.

The front door slammed, and I looked up.

Guess she'd gotten the message, because she was gone.

7

Mari

Fuck those Neanderthals. I didn't care if Dutch had just given me the best orgasm of my life. I wasn't there to be their new best friend, and if they couldn't even say hi to me during their stupid card game, their loss. I'd keep my head down, do as little cleaning as possible, and figure out how to get back to civilization.

And maybe I'd use *them* for a little sucky fucky. I wasn't easy, but I was prepared to have a little fun, myself. Why not? I'd never see them again once I was off Savage Mountain.

For the time being, however, I'd decided to take a little walk and enjoy the evening. I'd not explored the property except for what was immediately around the house, so I followed a little path lit by moonlight.

I wondered what Luci had told everyone at the

hospital. I mean, I could skate for a few days of not showing up, I had the vacation time built up. She'd probably say I had a death in the family or something. But eventually I'd be expected back at work. And if I didn't make it, I'd be fired. Not that it was hard for someone like me with an advanced nursing degree to find a new job, but still.

And what had become of the guy I'd hit? I mean, had I really killed another human being? Strangely, I didn't feel badly about it. The guy was trying to hurt my friend. But still, to think I'd killed someone.

Not the best feeling.

To be honest, I'd do it again, no matter who was being assaulted. Any guy tries something like that on my watch, he was going to pay.

I'd thought Dutch had kind of liked me when we got into the hot tub and started kissing and stuff, but the way he ran off when we were done messing around, it was as if he *wanted* to humiliate me.

I mean, who does that? So fucked up.

Maybe that was part of some plan of theirs. Keep the paid help in their place.

Well, little did they know, I could play that game, too. And, I had a gun and knife. So I was just as badass.

On second thought, I'd better put that crap back. If they found it missing, they'd come straight to me, and I had a feeling that would not be good.

As I walked along the soft path, I had to wonder, would I ever get home? Would I have to hide for the rest of my life? I'd gone to fucking nursing school, and worked my ass off. I wanted to take care of patients, not clean a mansion in the woods.

And what had they been talking about when Victor mentioned having been in the Special Forces with the other guys? Just what kind of work did they do? Dutch had taken down that guy at the truck stop pretty skillfully, and I'd witnessed it first hand. He knew what he was doing, no doubt. I wasn't sure whether I should be frightened, or feel like the safest girl in the world.

Voices in the distance caught my attention, rising and then falling. I stopped dead in my tracks. Weren't we the only ones up here?

I knew I shouldn't wander too far from the cabin, but I wanted to see if there was someone out there. I had to figure the place out.

I walked another fifteen minutes, but the voices seemed to fade as the wind picked up. Could it be there'd never been any voices, and that it had been the wind the entire time?

I stopped where I was.

I was at an intersection of multiple paths and I was pretty sure I knew which one to take back.

Pretty sure.

Or was I?

Okay, it was the path to the right. I was sure. I started down it, the wind growing louder, and the voices—if there'd ever been any—long gone. My hair whipped around my face, and I crossed my arms against the dropping temperature. I began to hustle back to the cabin to get inside and warm up.

I walked for ten minutes, and then twenty, but I still wasn't where I'd begun. I turned around, pissed at myself for taking the wrong path, and headed back to where I'd come from. As I did, a big, fat raindrop landed on my face.

Great. Just great. A storm was coming. Or, maybe it was already here.

And I was still outside, unsure of how to get back.

But I wasn't lost. No, I was *not* lost.

Shit. I was lost. There was no denying it.

Cripes. I'd escaped a hit man, and now I was going to eat it by taking a simple walk in the woods. How's that for irony? The universe was having a good laugh at my expense, just like the guys in the house probably were, too.

Fuck. What was it they said to do if you're lost in the woods? I tried to remember back to the staged nature shows I used to watch, where guys went out and camped and pretended to live off the land and such. But it had come out later they were all a bunch of fakes, and had never risked their lives or been in danger over anything.

Survivorman, was the show. That's what it was. So stupid.

But I thought back to the episode where the guy had gotten lost. Well, fake-lost, but I'd still filed away his solution, in case I was ever in a similar situation.

Instead of continuing to walk and getting further lost, stop where you are, and wait to be rescued.

Yeah right. Who's going to rescue me?

Nobody, that's who.

I found a large tree trunk, and sank down to the ground against it, wrapping my arms tightly around my legs. The warm hot tub of earlier in the afternoon was long forgotten, and the stress of running for my life for defending my friend was crawling over my skin once again. To distract myself, I thought about the rest of what I'd seen that day.

Things had just gotten weirder after the hot tub. Such as a woman coming in to cook dinner. I hadn't seen anyone other than the guys, then bam, there's Betty Crocker herself puttering over the stove. I almost fell over when I saw her. I mean, maybe I should have guessed it, because who would live in a house like that and cook for themselves?

But the whole setup was weird.

That and the woman, cripes if she didn't make my skin crawl. If looks could kill, I'd have ended up on the dinner table with some fava beans and a nice Chianti. She clearly hated me before I'd even said *hello*. Which was too bad because I wouldn't have minded a female friend.

There was more to the little Savage Mountain paradise than met the eye, that was for damn sure. I just had to remember to do my work, keep my head down, and keep my big trap shut.

I'd never been too good at that last one.

What had the cook's name been? Lee? Ann? Or maybe Leeann? She was a small woman, attractive if you took away the scowl she wore. She slammed pots and pan around while she cooked what turned out to be an incredibly delicious meal of roast chicken and vegetables.

But she sure didn't seem happy to be feeding the hired help, namely *me*, the brand new cleaning lady who didn't know as much as where the Windex was kept.

The rain, which I'd hoped was just going to be a few drops here and there, turned into a steady drizzle, stopping my reminisces. Because I was camped out under a tree, the water pooled on the leaves far above my head. When they couldn't hold the rain's weight any longer, the little buggers released their puddles onto my head with a rude, cold splash. I pulled my sweatshirt up over my face, another trick I'd seen on the survivor show, so my warm breath would keep at least the top of my body relatively heated. I wasn't shivering—yet. I knew when that kicked in, I'd be in big trouble.

I'd been an idiot for running out of the house like I had, my second big mistake in less than twenty-four hours.

I THOUGHT back to how over dinner, the cook had kept a close watch over the guys as they ate their meals and chatted among themselves. Like, a really close watch, both protective and possessive. No doubt she had the hots for at least one of them, and her glaring at me as if I were the new competition made it clear her crushes were not reciprocated.

Regardless, her dinner was amazing. And I was starving.

But instead of joining the guys at the dining table, my plate was set at the kitchen island counter where I thought Leeann would sit, too. But since I had cooties, apparently, she stood by the kitchen sink, shoveling food into her mouth directly from her cooking pans and glowering in my direction.

What was up her ass?

But just because I wasn't exactly dining with the guys didn't mean they weren't speaking to us. Or, at least, to me.

"Yo, Mari, how do you like the digs so far?" the perfectly barbered Victor asked from the table, pointing his fork at me before taking another mouthful of the delicious meat.

The watch cap he wore down to his eyebrows was the perfect contrast to his tidy facial hair, partially obscuring some of the most beautiful dimples I'd ever seen on a man.

Considering I had no real cleaning duties yet, and

that I was being fed like a queen, Savage Mountain had been quite the lovely vacation.

Even if I had to sit at the counter like a hired hand. Better than Cinderella.

So far, anyway.

Regardless, I smiled brightly and looked over at them.

"The mountain's amazing. Such a beautiful place. Really. Thank you again for…" I had to word this carefully, "letting me join the team."

Christ, I sounded like I was back at work. My *real* work, where I suppose I was a hired hand of a different type and where I could be a first-class suck up when the occasion required it.

But with this group I had a feeling I'd be sucking something else. At least I was starting to hope so.

Down girl.

A growl reminded me that the attention I'd received from the guys *really* pissed Leeann off. She began to slam dirty dishes into the sink, including mine.

"Hey, Leeann, I had a few more bites I was gonna—" I said, fork still in hand.

Red got up from the table to bring his plate to the sink. "Just ignore her, Mari. She's always in a shitty mood." He laughed, like it was funny.

Huh. That was the first time the gorgeous redheaded grandson of Ireland had said a thing to me. A tingle ran down my spine as he glanced my way, his strong chiseled jaw and slightly crooked nose causing a light sweat to break out on my forehead. A small spray of the sexiest freckles I'd ever seen was splashed across his nose.

Fuck me, he's as hot as my rescuers Dutch and Christian. Different, but just as sexy. Just like Victor.

It was also the first time I noticed he walked with a slight limp.

Good news followed. My cleaning duties did not include the dinner dishes. What a bonus—kitchen work was not high on the list of things I enjoyed doing, even for myself. So I disappeared to my room while Leeann made a racket that would wake the dead, until I heard the guys start a card game.

I loved cards and made my way back downstairs, jonesing for an invitation.

But an invitation didn't come. Apparently the hired help were not included in card games.

And that's how I came to be out in the woods.

THE RAIN BEGAN to come down harder, and pretty soon my survivor move of tucking my head and arms inside my shirt was doing no good. I had no idea what to do in the soaking rain.

Except pray to be rescued.

Out of the dark tempest, a hand unexpectedly shook my shoulder, scaring the shit out of me and sending my heart into my throat. Light shone from outside my sweatshirt, and when I peeked out, there were giant hiking boots right in front of me.

At least it wasn't a wild animal.

"Hey. Hey, wake up."

I pushed my head back through the neck of the shirt, and a blinding flashlight glowed right in my eyes. Instinctively I lifted my hand to cover them as I adjusted to the light.

"What? Who are you?" In my blindness, I felt for the tree behind me and started inching back up to my feet.

"Mari, it's me, Vic. We realized you were still out when it started raining."

A lump caught in my throat, and my voice cracked. "Really? You guys were looking for me?"

I realized I was full on shivering. Vic realized it too, and pulled his fleece shirt off, holding it out to me, leaving him in just a T-shirt.

"Yeah, of course. Why wouldn't we? Listen, take off that sweatshirt and put this on. C'mon, hurry."

I peeled my sweatshirt and undershirt off, which left me in my bra—also soaked.

"Take that off, too. I'll face the other way," he said, which he did. "You need to get all the wet items off your skin as fast as you can."

I obeyed and pulled on the fleece, magically warm from Vic's body heat. I instantly felt better, especially when I got a whiff of his scent—masculine, clean, with maybe the slightest touch of hard-work perspiration.

"Let's hustle," he said, giving me a wry smile. "The rain's getting worse."

I was still pretty damn wet, and now Victor was getting soaked. But I wasn't giving him back the shirt, not that he'd take it. It was his fault—everyone's really —that I was out there to begin with.

Right?

Okay, I needed to take responsibility for my own shit, but I was still going to revel in being rescued by this James Bond-ian hunk.

He bunched up my clothes in one hand, and extended his other to me. I took it gratefully, trying to act cool, my shivers giving me away.

With my free hand, I pulled the fleece up over my nose, pretending to be staying warm. In reality, I was gobbling up the scent embedded in his shirt, and thinking about how I could accidentally on purpose forget to return it to him.

8

VICTOR

I was certainly in the running for all-time idiots in history for giving Mari my fleece. Now I was fucking freezing and she had my shirt over her nose to keep extra warm. But I couldn't let her walk the mile it took to get back home completely soaked to the skin, when she'd already been outside for god knew how long.

She really did look kind of pathetic, her hair matted and stringy, raindrops running down her face. But I had to admit that as soon as she pulled on my fleece my dick said *hello* in a way it hadn't in far too long.

My shirt was too big on her, of course, hanging down past her thighs, the sleeves extending beyond her fingertips. But her tits filled out the top just enough to let you know that underneath that genderless piece of clothing was a full grown, and generously developed *woman*.

I pressed the talk button on my short-range radio, something we all carried around for general coms. "Guys. I found Mari. We're headed back to the house now."

One of the guys responded with a loud crackle. "Thanks, Vic. What are your coordinates?"

I looked at my watch and repeated our location, Mari's eyes widening. Guess she'd never seen a GPS watch before.

"Okay, good. You'll be here in about fifteen. RTB and we'll have the coffee ready when you get here. Mission complete."

A chorus of "Roger that," rang out.

Mari stopped in her tracks.

"What was that all about? Coordinates? Mission? Is this some kind of mountain man lingo?"

"C'mon, don't stop walking. We're both getting colder." I gripped her freezing hand, picking up the pace. "And yes. That's how we talk."

Mari didn't need to know where we'd learned military jargon, or any of the other skills the government had spent a lot of time and money teaching us.

Nor did she need to know what it was in my past that sent me over to the dark side—also known as the private contractor —where I'd been bombarded with offers to put to use the 'unique' skills I learned as a member of Special Ops to very lucrative use.

So Uncle Sam had paid for my expensive training, and I'd given him the middle finger first chance I got.

It was inevitable. How messed up was it that I was shot twice for my country, but couldn't afford a new pickup truck?

My time as a sniper in Baghdad had been short-lived. They usually rotated guys in and out of active patrols pretty quickly because the work was deadly… and gruesome.

Home on leave, I'd been at a baseball game. I'd been feeling okay, my team was getting their asses kicked, when suddenly everything just… blanked.

I woke up in a police car with no memory of how the hell I'd gotten there. The officers kindly informed me that some guy in front me at the game had snatched a foul ball from directly in front of me, and that I'd taken him down with my arm around his throat when he was a jerk about it.

I'd known that after the work I'd done I'd never really go back to 'normal life,' as they liked to call it, but I had no idea I'd become a walking, talking time bomb, ready to kill at the slightest provocation.

Thankfully, I was able to talk them into calling the Pentagon and my old CO vouched for me, and I got off. But after that, I was *done*. Safer for the whole world for me to just fade away into the wilderness. And I meant it, I was done.

Done at least until the last job we guys had taken in South America had almost gotten us killed.

Now I was *really* done.

The lights of the house shone ahead of Mari and me, and I didn't think I'd ever been so happy to see them. Not because I was miserable, wet, and freezing—that was nothing compared to some of the shit I'd been through—but I had to get back inside and clear my head of all thoughts of work.

That was why we loved long, drawn-out card games. Talking with my brothers, even if it was just shooting the shit and busting each others' chops, kept the waking nightmares at bay.

"Well, there they are," Christian said, holding up a glass of what looked like scotch. "Want some?"

"Oh hell, yeah. Screw the coffee," I said, stripping myself of wet clothes down to my skivvies in the kitchen to avoid making a mess of the house.

Mari watched me, but didn't seem interested in doing the same. Couldn't blame her. As sexy as she was, it'd be like raw meat being tossed in front of a pack of hungry Rottweilers.

"Hey Christian, can I have a scotch, too?" she asked.

"Sure," he said. "Or would you rather have brandy?"

Her eyes lit up like she'd been offered a million bucks. "Oh my god, *yes.*"

"Tell ya what," I said, turning her to me. "You go up to your room and get clean and dry, and I'll bring you a brandy. How's that sound?"

"Yes, please!" she said, running for the stairs. I watched her ass bounce up the steps.

I looked forward to bringing her a nightcap.

As soon as she was gone though, Dutch asked, "What the hell was she doing out there?"

I shook my head while I topped off my scotch. "No idea. But she was nearly hypothermic, half asleep because of it. She wouldn't have gotten through the night."

Christian rolled his eyes. "You'd think a nurse would have more sense than to go wandering in strange woods after dark. With rain on the way? Girl needs to learn."

Yeah, we had a few things to teach her, and I had a feeling she might be a challenging student.

AFTER HEADING UPSTAIRS, I knocked on Mari's bedroom door. "Hey. Can I come in?"

I heard some rustling, and footsteps approaching.

"Hi," she said, pulling the door open. Her hair was freshly washed and hung around her shoulders in long, wet ropes and she'd obviously dug up some clothes to wear. She was fresh and clean, and my carnal side was dying to get my hands on her.

"Here's your brandy."

"Oh, thank you so much," she said, sipping the drink. "Wow... this is perfect. Come on in. As you can see, I have my very own seating area."

She gestured toward a corner of her room that

did, indeed, look very inviting with two overstuffed chairs, a small sofa, and a coffee table. It was all in white, just like the rest of the room. Very girly and feminine, just like her. It was like a lucky match made in heaven.

"Isn't this room amazing?" she said, her eyes wide open as she looked around. "Much nicer than even my apartment at home," she said with a laugh, settling back into her chair and taking a sip of her brandy like she didn't have a care in the world. "You guys musta been anticipating me somehow."

I set the scotch I'd brought with me on the table between us. "I'm glad you like it. It is a nice room."

She leaned forward to put her drink down too, giving me a nice peek inside her zip-up hoodie, which was not really zipped up all that high.

Focus, buddy.

"Tell me, Vic, how is it that you guys have a house with a guest room done up like this? I mean, this is clearly a woman's room."

Of course she was the type to ask nosy-ass questions. Christian and Dutch had warned me. And anyone who wanders off in the woods by herself after dark is not always going to have the best judgment.

"Well, I think the guys told you we all used to be in the military?"

She nodded, her attention rapt. Christ it had been a long time since I'd spoken with a beautiful woman. I'd forgotten how nice it was to spend time with one. Shit,

I'd forgotten how nice it was to even look at one, that's how long it had been.

"When we got out, we bought this place. It came with all the furniture, thanks to the folks who sold it to us."

She looked around with approval. "This must have been a girl's room. Is that where the clothes come from in the dresser and closet?"

"Not sure where they came from, to be honest. The last owners left all sorts of things behind. Or, they might have been left by our last maid."

The expression on her face shifted the smallest amount, then snapped back to her brilliant smile.

Was I not supposed to say 'maid'? Oops.

"We go to town every so often. Next time we do, you can get some new clothes," I told her, hoping to change the subject. "It sounds like the guys rescued you from a bad situation on their way up here."

She bit her bottom lip, nodding. "They did. I am very lucky. But now, I don't know what to do about the people after me. I don't think they could track me here, but I do worry about my next step. Like, will I ever get to go home?"

She looked out the window into the dark, I guess trying to imagine what her new life might look like, if she had to forge one. With her feet tucked under her, she wrapped her arms around herself and looked incredibly small and vulnerable. I wanted to hold her, half for me, but also for her.

"Are you cold?" I asked.

She nodded. "A little, I guess. But the brandy is kicking in nicely."

I stood, and held out a hand. "C'mon. Let me put you to bed. You had a big scare, and I don't want you catching a cold."

She stood, drink in hand, and headed to the four-poster bed covered in a fluffy white down comforter. I peeled the covers back for her and studied her face.

"Thanks for saving me tonight," she said as she lay down. "I'm sorry for the trouble I caused."

She reached for my hand, holding it tightly.

"Well, you had us worried. We don't need a dead nurse on our hands."

I took her drink and set it on the nightstand. Then I took both her hands.

"I'm glad you're here. We all are, actually," I said.

She shrugged shyly. "It didn't seem like it earlier."

She was right. We didn't welcome new people into our circle. It didn't matter how beautiful they were.

"Don't take it personally. We're not really good with the mushy stuff." It was all I could say. And, I wasn't in her room to talk, anyway.

Slowly, I moved my hands up her arms, bringing my fingers to the zipper on her hoodie. I wanted to give her time to tell me to fuck off, if she were so inclined. But I didn't think she was.

Turned out I was right. She'd just had the shit

scared out of her again, and seemed hungry for some affection. She licked her lips, and smiled.

I eased the zip down until her hoodie fell open, displaying some of the most gorgeous tits I'd ever seen. Heavy and full, with brown upturned nipples, the kind that were crafted by the gods themselves. I brought my hands under them to gently pull them together and up to my hungry lips.

She didn't say a word, but her eyes fluttered closed and the sweetest sigh escaped her lips as I took one in my mouth. I rolled my tongue around her hard point, teasing her warm skin.

I moved over to the other breast and when they were both nice and wet, I pulled back to look at them, smooth and shiny. I knew exactly what I wanted to do. But would she let me?

In one swift move, I slipped her sweat pants down her slim hips and dropped them on the floor.

As I lay her on the bed, she asked, "What about you?"

She looked me up and down with a smile, and I decided to be a little playful.

"What about me?"

She laughed and pulled my T-shirt over my head, then going straight for the fly on my jeans. In moments, I was just as naked as she, my rock-hard dick bouncing between the two of us.

"Nice," she said, stroking me with her soft hand. Her touch, while light, was also strangely electric. It was all I could do not to shoot my load right then and there.

"You like it, pretty girl?" I asked, twirling chunks of her nearly dry hair around my fingers. I was dying to bury my hands in her tresses and pull her down on my cock, but I knew better than to be an animal, hard as it was to resist the temptation.

But I didn't need to direct her. She slid to her knees right in front of me, opening her lips enough to take just my head, and savor the shiny drop of precum I had for her.

She looked up at me with her magical eyes. "Tastes nice."

Turning back to my dick, she engulfed the head, creating a suction around my rim that caused me to draw in a deep breath.

Focus, focus. *Do not come yet.*

"I'm gonna suck you," she said softly.

That was all it took.

I wove my fingers through her hair to grip her head, and followed her movement as she gradually took me down her throat.

Holy fuck.

I watched myself disappear into her mouth all the way to my balls.

Cripes, did they teach that in nursing school? If so, I was hooked.

She pistoned on my dick, slowly gathering speed. My balls tightened with sweet agony.

"Fuck, baby, I'm gonna come. I'm gonna come in your mouth."

Well, she must have liked the sound of that because the woman doubled down on me, sucking so hard I could have shot my cum across the room if she hadn't been there to receive it. I came like a machine-gun, so hard I had to hold the bedpost to keep from bouncing off the mattress. I didn't want to miss a second of what she was giving me.

She somehow managed to swallow all my seed, and instead of *my* putting *her* to bed, she pulled the covers back and pulled me in after her.

"Will you spend the night with me?" she asked in a sweet voice.

If she didn't cut it out, I'd be hard again in minutes.

"Hell yes," I said.

9

MARI

Vic reached for my brandy on the nightstand, helped himself to a sip, and passed it to me.

And I froze.

"What… is that… on your back?"

I prayed it wasn't what I thought it was, but my stomach churned anyway. The thick, twisted flesh was too well known from my experience in the nursing world. But never had I see it so hideously deformed before.

Vic, though, lay back, hands behind his head like he didn't have a care in the world. I guess at that moment, he didn't.

"I was beaten," he said simply, looking to gauge my reaction.

And, there it was. The punch to the gut I'd been hoping to avoid.

My mouth was dry as a bone, but I managed to squeak out a few words. "Can I see it again?"

"Sure." He turned on his side, facing away from me. Again, the bile rose in my throat, but I forced it down to look at him.

Long, ropey lines of raised flesh crisscrossed his back. The scars looked old, but no doubt had inflicted a kind of agony that would never be forgotten. The only time I'd ever seen anything like it was in a horror movie.

"You were beaten? By whom? And where?"

He turned over to face me and took my hand, obviously moved by my concern.

"I was captured by the enemy. That's really all I can tell you," he said quietly.

I nodded slowly. "Okay. So it was a military thing?"

He leaned forward and kissed my forehead. "Yes, it was. Now let's get some sleep. I have to get up early."

"You do? Why?"

He rolled his eyes at me, chuckling before he reached for the light. "You ask too many questions."

He kissed me on the forehead and got comfortable, never letting go of my hand.

It felt so good to have someone protective right by my side, but the terror of being chased came flooding back to me as Victor drifted off and I lay staring at the ceiling in the darkness.

I would have gotten up to read or something—that's what I always did when I had insomnia, but I didn't want to wake him, he was sleeping so soundly and smelled so good.

Instead, a hundred thoughts raced through my mind, the way they do at night when there are no other distractions.

Being up at the cabin with four gorgeous men was all well and good, but I couldn't stay there indefinitely. First off, I'd already had sex with two of them, not something I'd normally do, but the last twenty-four hours of my life had been anything but normal. And the guys were all so damned gorgeous.

I didn't want there to be drama among them, though. I had enough of that to deal with when I got back to the real world. I mean, I had a life. Friends, a job, an apartment, a car. Responsibilities...

What if I hadn't killed that guy? What would have happened to Luci?

I couldn't even contemplate it.

The question was, how would I get the gangbangers off my back? Was that even possible?

Everything I knew told me that no, they weren't going away. At least not until they made me pay.

"MARI! Get up! You have work to do!"

Bam, bam, bam.

I sat straight up in bed in my pretty mountain room, light streaming through the shutters on my French doors.

I was alone. No Victor.

The banging repeated, and I blinked, trying to get my head straight and failing.

What was going on? Was the damn house on fire?

"Who is it?" I called, running my hand through my hair.

And what the hell time was it?

I heard a big sigh outside my door and knew it was Leeann. "You need to get your ass out of bed and downstairs to help with breakfast."

Footsteps retreated from my room, becoming fainter until they clomp-clomped down the stairs.

Okay. Well, at least my head's clear, and good morning to you too, Leeann.

So I had to help with breakfast? I was cool with that. I liked breakfast, and I could cook it quite well, having successfully paid for a good deal of my nursing school working in the hospital kitchen. Finding some clothes to throw on, I quickly washed up, and hustled down the stairs.

"Leeann, if you needed my help, why didn't you tell me last night so I could have gotten up early?" I asked when I got to the kitchen.

Instead of giving me an answer, Leeann just scowled at me. "Chop these onions. Then make scrambled eggs, using the entire dozen over there."

"All righty then," I mumbled, and got to work.

A big greasy pan clattered to the floor right next to my foot.

"Christ, Leeann, be more careful. That nearly hit me."

Her face was half sneer, half homicidal disdain as her right nostril lifted in a very ugly expression. "Clean that pan. Then clean the floor," she spat. "Then you can cook."

Okayyy. Getting the Cinderella vibe again, but it was all good. It wasn't like I'd be stuck on the mountain for the rest of my life. Most likely only for a few days, max. Right?

I got down on my hands and knees to clean up the bacon grease from the pan Leeann had 'accidentally' dropped. That's why, when the guys filed in for breakfast from wherever they'd been, they didn't see me behind the kitchen counter.

"Hey Leeann, good morning."

It was Victor's voice, so I bounced up to my feet.

"Hey Vic. How'd you sleep?" I asked with a little smile.

The guys just looked at each other, and Leeann rolled her eyes. They sat, and she pulled more bacon out of the oven.

Victor said nothing.

I stood there like an idiot, looking from one person to the next. Okay, there was something about this little group I had yet to figure out.

What was with these guys? Victor was acting just like Dutch had, when he abruptly left me at the hot tub after we'd messed around.

And then later in the night, they couldn't be bothered to talk to me.

Bunch of assholes, that's what they were, even if Victor had found me in the woods, huddled under a tree.

"Leeann, what else can I do to help?"

Maybe if I played my cards right, *she'd* talk to me?

"Cut the melon over there," she said, gesturing with her shoulder. She handed me a huge knife.

"Sure." I set up my chopping area right next to her.

"Hey, so how long have you been up here?" I asked, trying to catch her eye.

She glanced over at me, filling me with a hope that was instantly dashed.

"Put the melon in that bowl," she said, pointing. "One inch chunks."

That was all I got. Yup, I had to get the hell out of there.

LEEANN DISAPPEARED without a word halfway through cleaning the breakfast dishes. The guys were long gone, having run off to whatever it was they did with their days as rich, apparently retired mountain men.

I doubted they were out chopping wood or hunting

for their suppers, unless they wanted to. As fancy as the cabin was, and as good as the food was, I didn't get the feeling too much roughing it was going on.

So I just cleaned the rest of what had been used for breakfast in the kitchen by myself.

I was a sweaty mess when I'd finished, seeing as the kitchen was huge and Leeann had used nearly every pot or pan during her meal preparation. Perfect opportunity to try out the gorgeous outdoor shower I'd spotted when I'd first arrived.

There wasn't another soul in sight as I headed outside with a towel I'd found in my bathroom. The quiet was actually kind of nice and the tension from earlier was slowly seeping from my bones.

Fuck those jerks. Did they think I was just going to be their little fuck-maid? Work, fuck, sleep, work, fuck, sleep?

I mean, not that I had anything against fucking them. Sure, I was letting my freak flag fly, but I deserved it. I was coming off a hell of a dry spell, and if I was going to spend a few days with four hot guys… well, I might as well make the most of it.

I also didn't mind cleaning their house, at least for the short term. But they'd better wise up and treat me with some respect, or some asses were going to get kicked.

I pushed a couple spider webs out of the way, and closed the swinging door behind me. It was a beautiful teak set-up with a wooden floor, two shower heads, and built-in benches on each side. There was even a tree growing in the corner, the stall having been built around it, which gave the whole thing a slightly naughty but wholesome natural vibe to it. It was quite the little paradise.

Not that the rest of the 'cabin' was lacking in any way.

I hung my clothes and towel in the corner and let the pulsing, heavy jets massage my scalp. The flow, while if it had been any harder would have certainly started to ache after a few minutes, was the perfect pressure for washing my thick hair.

As I reached for the soap, the shower's wooden door creaked open.

"Who is that?" I shrieked, folding my soapy arms in front of me.

"Relax, Mari. It's just me." Red released a towel from his waist, hanging it in the corner over mine.

His beautiful asscheeks flexed as he did, but it was when he turned around that my legs felt weak. I reached for the shower wall to steady myself and watch him walk toward me. My gaze started at the huge cock bouncing against his thigh and moved up past the V that led to his washboard abs, which lead to his broad pecs, covered in the slightest spray of chest hair.

In red. All his hair was red. And he was fucking gorgeous.

Still.

I got my voice back. "Um, Red, I was showering. Do

you think you could let me finish, alone, and come back when I'm done?"

He smiled, damn him, with his chiseled jaw, crooked nose, and insane sleeve tattoos.

"How's the water?"

Okay, I know the guy didn't talk much, but it would be really nice if he could engage about the current shower situation. Just this one time.

"Red? Can you please leave?" I had one hand across my boobs, and the other blocking my ladybits. Both of which were starting to feel rather… warm.

Apparently he thought my pose was hilarious, because his grin grew wider, and his cock actually twitched for me.

"Just relax, Nursey," he said quietly, as he stepped under the shower to wet his hair.

What the fucking fuck? Did he have some sort of hearing problem? And I was not his *Nursey.*

But if he wanted to play it like that, fine. I'd just finish my shower and get the hell out.

These guys sure knew how to make a girl feel welcome. Or at least feel like a member of the family.

Wait a second… family… I grew up with a bunch of cousins and was a pro at defending myself. I stepped into the shower spray, braced myself, and shoulder-chucked Red as hard as I could.

He stumbled back, dropping his soap.

Take that.

"Damn. You could knock a guy over with that move."

"Oh? Did I bump you? Sorry." I soaped myself as fast as I could, my back to him. He'd already seen enough, and my ass was the least embarrassing option I had left.

And rinsing would take only a few seconds.

"I'm not going to try anything. I just thought we could share the shower," he said in his low voice.

He might not have much to say, but he had some pretty big nerve to help himself to my shower time.

"Well you thought wrong," I said, moving more quickly.

"Hey," he said quietly, his voice sounding different and slowing my movements some. "Seriously. I'm not a jerk. Let me help."

Taking the bar of soap, he stood behind me and ran it over my shoulder, then down my arm. When he reached my hand, he intertwined his fingers with mine and his cock bounced against my ass.

And it was a very hard cock.

10

RED

"Doesn't that feel nice, Nursey?" I asked, rubbing the soap over Mari's beautifully smooth skin. She was silk and satin, more so than anyone I'd ever touched.

"Wh... why do you keep calling me *Nursey*?" she stammered.

Every extra inch of her I soaped made her quiver even more.

I chuckled. Couldn't help it. I hadn't come into the shower to mess with her. But now, well, things were different. She was responding.

To *me*. A pleasant surprise.

I'd admired her from afar since the first day she'd landed in our little world, when we made her eat dinner at the kitchen counter. I knew the other guys were drooling over her, too, much as we all tried to play it cool.

She wasn't just a gorgeous woman. She had self-respect, too. *That* got me.

I swept the long wave of hair clinging to her skin and threw it forward over her shoulder. As soon as her neck was exposed, my lips were on her, and damn if her skin wasn't both soft and electric at the same time.

How did she do that?

I clasped her fingers, wrapping my other arm around her to cup the gorgeous breasts I'd been eyeing since she'd arrived on the mountain. Lingering on her nipples until they were rock hard, I enjoyed their slippery goodness, kneading and playing.

"Damn, these babies," I growled, grinding my cock against her pert cheeks.

People said I was shy. But was I? I'd never been sure. I just didn't have a lot to say. I preferred to speak once and be sure about what I was saying rather than blab like a dumbass and have to retread my steps.

People mistook that for weakness all the time, much to their detriment. I was like that snake you never saw until he had his fangs in you.

So yeah, when it came to sex, when I decided to go for it, I was pretty fucking aggressive. That's just how I was, and I hoped Mari would respond to me exactly the way she was. But you never know how these things will go. If the girl wasn't down with your advances, game over.

Booyah.

Running the soap over her stomach and across her belly button towards her waist and core, I gently built up a little lather. As I got closer to the goods, her legs separated to offer me better access. She squirmed under my touch and I found her pussy juicy and wet, and not just from the shower.

Unable to hold back any longer, I spun her around to face me.

"Put your leg up on the bench there," I said, pointing. Biting her lip, she nodded. She gripped my shoulder for balance, her new position leaving her with one foot on the floor, and the other propped up, leaving her open and exposed.

I ran a finger through her slick folds, and surprised her by bringing my lips to hers in a roughly tender kiss, igniting a crazy hunger where we couldn't get enough of each other. I'd initially thought our encounter was about nothing more than getting our rocks off, but our soulful, exploring kiss became more urgent by the moment. It had been too long since I'd touched a woman, but I was okay with that. I could deal with long dry spells. But this one had invaded my dreams every night since I first saw her.

With one hand between her spread legs, I ran a finger over her engorged clit, my other hand on her lower back, pulling her into me to the point of taking her breath away.

"I'm going to shave your pussy now," I said matter of factly.

"Wha…?" she mumbled, lust drunk. "My pussy?"

What could I say? Shaving women was one of my kinks.

I reached for the razor and shave cream under my towel and turned to her with one in each hand. I'd brought them for myself… but they could easily do double duty.

The look of surprise on her face was worth the price of admission.

She leaned against the wall, obeying silently and wide-eyed, trusting me with her most sensitive of parts. When I brought the razor to her swollen lips after applying a thin layer of shave cream, I gently and carefully dragged it in short, repetitive strokes. She gasped, but I could see the flush in her skin. She was getting off on it as much as I was.

She was already neatly trimmed, so it wouldn't take long to shave her, but I was pretty sure she'd never gone bare before. This was going to be a treat for us both.

The water beat down on us, and she kept pushing back the dark hair the water carried to her face, showing off those glittering green eyes.

Crouched as I was before her, I reached to stroke my raging dick, which was ready to explode with her pussy right in my face.

Calm down, dude. Ladies first.

"There," I said, finishing up, studying the perfect petals revealed to my eyes. "So soft and smooth."

Her hands slid down her taut belly to feel skin that had never been bare. At the first touch she gasped.

"Do you like it?" I asked.

She kept smoothing her fingers over her velvety lips, her breath shuddering in and out. "Yeah. They're so soft and sensitive."

I stroked her naked pussy lips, my dick begging for some attention.

"I'm going to fuck you now."

She gave me a gorgeous smile, full of mischief.

Yes.

I turned her to face away and pushed her forward so she was bent in half over the bench. Without a word, she spread her legs wider and arched to open herself to me.

"Hell, yes," I said, nudging her ankles slightly apart to get her in just the right position. "You ready, baby?"

After she nodded, I entered her slowly and deliberately until I could go no further, my cock stretching her inner walls to their limit. She moaned, the lustful sound guiding me until I was all the way in. Fuck she was tight, and I pulled back just as slowly before thrusting all the way.

Reaching back between her legs, she gripped my balls, nearly driving me over my goddamned edge. I wouldn't last long at that rate.

"Fuuuck… " I yelled, pulling back. I started

pistoning her, my hands gripping her waist for purchase. And she loved it. Her tits hung heavy, bouncing forcefully at my thrusting.

"Yes, yes, yes," she yelled, pounding her free hand on the bench and pushing against me for more. Her fingers dug into the wet wood of the shower stall as I slammed home and her orgasm rushed over her, mine joining seconds later.

Through her screams I called her name, her real name—not Nursey, as I'd teased her with before.

As I slowed, her legs buckled, dislodging me as she sank to her knees and onto the floor. I reached to turn off the shower and grabbed a huge towel, which I wrapped her with, pulling her to the shower bench. After I'd draped a towel around my waist, I pulled her into the crook of my arm as we caught our breath.

After ten or fifteen minutes—who knew, maybe it had been longer—I helped her stand, and we gradually made our way back to the house.

With my arm supporting a good deal of her weight, my slightly unsteady gait was more obvious than usual.

"Hey, Red," she said softly.

"Yeah?"

My knee stiffened as we climbed the steps to the cabin.

"Why do you limp?" she asked.

I'd been waiting for that question. And maybe someday I'd share the whole story with her.

But not that day.

"War injury." I wasn't ready to tell her the whole story, but then again there were a lot of stories on Savage Mountain. Enough to last a lifetime.

When we reached her bedroom door, I gave her a kiss on the cheek.

"Red? Can I tell you something?" she asked, turning at the door.

Christ, I hope she didn't have more nosy questions. Sexy as fuck, but this woman was nosier than the CIA.

"Yup."

"When I arrived a few days ago, I snagged a gun and knife out of the car's glove box for, you know, just in case."

Oh for Christ's sake. We'd been looking for those things all over the place, I was about ready to chew Christian and Dutch's asses over their poor weapon security. It was the sort of shit that got people killed.

Why hadn't it occurred to us to ask Mari if she'd seen them?

The answer was simple. Because she didn't seem like a knife and gun kind of girl.

"You know, we were searching for those things."

She looked down, embarrassed. "I'm sorry. I'd just arrived and was scared and didn't know what to expect. Let me get them for you."

She scurried into her room and grabbed the weapons from under her bed, where they were wrapped in a towel.

"Here," she said, handing the whole bundle to me.

I took them, angry, but not at her, for some reason I couldn't explain. "Thanks."

I turned and headed to my own room, leaving her in the doorway watching me walk away.

I liked her, probably too much. But that wouldn't get in the way of keeping things professional.

At least for the time being.

"HEY, here comes Red, you old dirty dog," Christian said, leaning back in his easy chair with a shit-eating grin.

"Chill out asshole," I said, settling into my own chair and pulling open a two-week old newspaper. "Dude, I fucking hate these old newspapers," I said, throwing it on the table. "Who the fuck cares what some asshole did this long ago? About the only decent thing in here are the goddamn comics."

Dutch shook his head, probably because I'd made the same bitch a thousand times before. "Then read the news online like everyone else does in the twenty-first century."

Christian continued to smile at me. "Mari is *nice*, isn't she?"

I nodded. I wasn't going to let him rile me. She was nice and so much more. "Amazing. Pretty, sexy, curious. Can't clean worth a damn, but what are you going to do?"

Everybody laughed.

We normally put more thought into bringing someone in to work for us, but I had the feeling Christian and Dutch were thinking with their little heads the day they'd brought her up the mountain. Sure, she'd been in a desperate situation, but we weren't knights in shining white armor waiting to save pretty girls. In our world, Lancelot got his ass killed, not rewarded.

We had other jobs to do. Important and dangerous jobs.

That paid us very handsomely.

But hey, I was not complaining.

To be honest, I'd be surprised if she stuck around for long. The woman had a life and career at home and probably just looked at us as a vacation and a good time. We'd be her one story of how she messed around with four mountain men, something she'd never do again. She'd meet a guy at the hospital, probably a doctor, settle down, and push out some kids.

And be bored as shit.

But I got a kick out of her, no lie. Maybe too much of a kick, because she was getting past my mental armor too quickly.

To hell with the cleaning, it wasn't all that bad. The way she tried to be part of the gang, and wasn't discouraged when we gave her the douchebag treatment turned me on.

I knew the other guys felt the same way.

I chose my words carefully. "I appreciate you guys bringing her up here. She's really cool."

Victor joined us and nodded. "I wouldn't mind getting to know her better. I mean, not just physically. But we all know that wouldn't be a good idea."

He said it like it was a half question, and looked from one to the other of us, waiting for someone to nod in agreement.

He was right, much as I hated to admit it. It wouldn't do to get attached, lovely as she was. For now, we could have fun with her if she was on board, and keep our noses to the grindstone.

"Hey, you guys think we might be able to do something about her little gang problem at home?" I asked.

My partners in crime all slowly nodded.

I knew they'd be on board.

NEXT MORNING, our cook Leeann cornered me in the kitchen before I sat down for breakfast.

"Um, Red, I have something to tell you. Something important," she said, wiping her hands on her apron.

It was strange to hear her voice, she spoke so little.

"What's up Leeann?"

She frowned and picked at her chewed-up cuticles. I hoped she wasn't going to revisit her proposal of a couple months previous. She wasn't my type, and that was all there was to it.

Leeann and me? Not gonna happen. Ever.

"I wasn't sure what to do about this, so I thought I'd just tell you," she said.

"What? What's going on Leeann?"

"The new girl—"

"Her name is Mari." None of us had missed the fact that Leeann wasn't happy about another woman on the premises, much less a woman who looked like Mari. Leeann wasn't ugly, but just… not a match. Never had there been a spark with her like there was with Mari.

And Leeann knew it. She'd carried a torch for me and I suspect all the guys, and that torch now burned bright with envy over the new girl in her territory. Never let anyone tell you that it's only the men who get possessive and territorial. Women are just as bad, and they fight just as dirty.

"Yeah. Her. Well, she stole something from the house."

No way. Mari?

"Ask her. The silver box from Persia. It's been missing for a couple days. I'd seen her looking at it, and then I went to her room where I found it hidden. I heard you guys talking about how great she was, and I thought you should know."

I remembered having seen Mari look over the Persian box, but then she'd been curious about all the artifacts we'd brought back from our world travels.

Mari? Sticky fingers?

Hmmm. I had to check, but I wasn't convinced.

"All right, Leeann. I'll take care of it. Thank you for letting me know."

Her hand lingered on my arm a bit too long.

"Okay, Red. I'm sorry I snooped in her room, but I just knew she'd taken it."

The other guys were filing down the stairs for breakfast.

"Next time just come to us. Don't go into anyone else's room."

Her mouth dropped open. "But, Red, I was just trying to—"

"Do you understand me, Leeann?" We did not need any drama, especially of the female variety.

She turned and scurried back to the stove.

Before Mari came down, I quickly briefed the guys on what Leeann had told me. They were understandably concerned, but had the same thoughts I did.

"I'll be honest Red, I wouldn't say yay or nay on this without talking to Mari," Vic said. "Leeann's… well, let's just talk to Mari."

I agreed, and dove into my breakfast.

"Hey, Mari, could you come over here?" I asked when she came down, getting nods from the guys.

Almost achingly, her face lit up at the possibility of being included in a conversation. Was she really that lonely? "Hi guys. How's everyone this morning?"

She was dying to pull up a seat and hang with us, I could tell. And it made me feel kind of shitty.

"Mari, we understand that something valuable is

missing from the household, and that it's in your room," Christian said, his voice quiet and firm but friendly. I swear, he would have made a great cop if he'd wanted to.

She looked at us happily, oblivious to the trouble she might be in. "Oh, right, I did borrow that old *Sports Illustrated*. Does someone need it back?" She looked at each of us with a question mark on her face. "Sorry, I thought it was okay to take to my room."

I looked around the table, and could see the guys were behind me on this. "No Mari, we're talking about something else. Something *valuable*."

"What is it?" She wrinkled her nose. "What's missing? And how would it be in my room?"

I seriously doubted anything was in her room, but I had to ask. We all did.

"Mari, can we go up to your room to look for the silver box from Persia?" I asked.

"Yeah but the Persian box is right over there—"

She pointed to the empty spot where it usually was. "Oh. That's funny. It was there the other day."

"Did you take it Mari?"

"What do you mean, take it? Jeez, what would I do with a silver box? I don't have any jewelry to put in it," she said with a laugh. "I'm happy to help you look for it though, if you like."

Christian stood. "Mari, can we go up to your room to look for the box?"

"Well, yeah. Help yourselves. Are you saying you

think I took it?" she asked, realization dawning on her face. "Why would you think that? Surely you guys know I have bigger problems on my mind than swiping your travel souvenirs."

We stood, and Christian kept his voice calm and friendly.

"C'mon. Let's go to your room."

11

MARI

Standing there in the dining room, only one thought was on my mind... were they fucking kidding me?

They thought I *stole* something? From their house?

Incredulous, I looked from one face to the other, and they basically looked back at me emotionlessly. Serious as a heart attack.

It was too much to take.

First they ignore me, except for when they manage to get me naked.

Not that I was complaining. Three sessions of knee-buckling orgasms definitely earned my appreciation.

But then they accuse me of stealing? I'm on the fucking run from some gangbangers. Stealing shit was the absolutely last thing on my mind.

"Okay, guys. Let's go upstairs. All of you." I gestured at the four of them. When they were a little slow, I turned on my 'nurse voice'. The one I used when patients were being pains in the ass. "C'mon. Now."

I no longer cared if I was in the one-down position because I was their fucking cleaning lady.

They'd whacked the wrong hornet's nest.

Was that a smirk on Red's face?

"What do you think is so funny, over there?" I demanded, scowling at him. "You wanna say something, say it."

His face went serious, and he shook his head sternly. "All right, Mari. Take off the boxing gloves. Let's go upstairs and get this over with."

Oh, my high and mighty military friends.

Not.

I stormed up the stairs with Dutch practically up my ass, as if I were going to escape.

Escape. Ironically, that was exactly what I wanted to do at that moment. Escape from my whole fucking life.

Before I could open my bedroom door, Christian stepped in front of me and placed his hand on the knob. "You know, Mari. If we find you've stolen from us, there will be a price to pay."

I rolled my eyes, and stared right back into his face.

He'd even tried to talk 'nice' the whole time, like that excused his assholery.

"Christian, are you trying to make me laugh? Because you're doing a good job."

Dutch got in my face, as if playing the bad cop. "You think this is funny? We save you, take you in, and you steal from us?"

I glanced at Victor, hoping for some solidarity since he was the only one who'd not spoken yet.

But he looked equally as stern. Actually, kind of pissed, too. "This isn't a lark. I really hope you didn't do this."

Welcome to crazy town.

"Go," I demanded, gesturing toward the door with my head.

Wait till the next time one of them wanted some nookie. Have fun with your blue balls, motherfucker!

"Okay guys, sweep the premises," Christian said, holding me by the upper arm as if I'd try to get away.

"Yeah, go for it guys. Because you won't find a goddamn thing."

I tried to wriggle out of Christian's grip, but his giant palm pretty much encircled my arm.

Which just incensed me more.

"You have a lot of nerve, accusing me. I am a nurse. An educated professional. I have a nice income and a nice apartment. The idea that I'd need to steal from you is beyond absurd. After your stupid search turns up nothing, I'm leaving. I've had it with this freakshow you run here—"

Christian's grip on my arm tightened. "It would be in your best interest to shut up right now, Mari."

No. Fucking. Way.

But I decided to stay quiet. Let the assholes make fools of themselves and apologize to me later.

Yeah, they could lick my boots. I was looking forward to that.

So I tapped my foot on the floor. Loudly.

Christian turned to me and sighed. "Have you ever heard the term, *the lady doth protest too much?*"

"Yeah, I have. Thanks, Shakespeare."

He looked down, shaking his head.

Victor suddenly stopped rummaging. "Guys. Check this out."

It was the stupid fucking Persian box.

In one of my dresser drawers.

"Oh, that's bullshit," I cried. "I've never even looked in that drawer. All my things are in the top drawers."

Victor approached me, holding the box at eye level. "This is how you thank us? You steal from us?"

I looked at Red, hoping for some help. But he, too, glared at me.

Guess I was on my own.

"Let go of me," I yelled, attempting to yank free of Christian. "I'm out of here."

Christian started walking me toward the bed. "This is not cool, Mari."

He threw me down, where I lay, stunned.

Then the guys filed out the door and locked it behind themselves without another word.

So now I was a prisoner.

I pounded on the door. "C'mon guys, I didn't steal that thing. You're being ridiculous."

But all I heard were footsteps getting fainter and fainter.

AFTER WHAT SEEMED LIKE HOURS, my bedroom door flew open.

Unfortunately, it flew open at the exact same time I was attempting to lower myself out my bedroom window using the bed sheets I'd tied together. I think I'd seen that in some movie. Funny thing was, it never worked in the movies.

Guess it wasn't going to work for me, either.

Christian and Dutch stood looking at me with a mixture of annoyance and amusement on their faces as I froze, one leg out the window, my ass still poking back into the room.

Before I could really test out my escape plan, there were four strong hands pulling me back in the house.

Dutch reached into his pocket and pulled out some colorful rope, the kind I'd seen at REI, where they sold it by the yard. Christian pulled a knife out of his pocket, and flicked open a blade. Dutch tossed the rope to him. He cut two long pieces and tossed them back.

Then they tied me, by the wrists, to the bedposts.

"You can't imprison me! You're going to pay for this. Victor! Red!" I screamed, hoping the other guys would rescue me.

I tugged on the ropes to no avail. There was some slack, but not enough to reach the actual knots. Dutch sat on the edge of the bed, now bare of sheets because of my brilliant plan to escape out the window.

"Vic and Red are in agreement on your guilt. Don't bother hollering for them. My question is, how the hell did you think you'd get away with this?"

"Oh fuck off, Dutch. And I don't like lying on the bare mattress," I said, squirming. "Seriously, you four are fucking mental if you think I did this."

The guys looked at each other and then back at me.

"Doesn't look like you can do much about it," he said, shrugging. He looked at his watch. "It's time for your punishment."

"Punishment for stealing that stupid box, which I didn't actually steal? The fucker is ugly. No way I'd have that piece of shit in my house. Guys, seriously!"

Christian loosened my ropes.

Oh, thank god. They were coming to their senses.

Rubbing my wrists, I started to sit up.

Before I could, Christian flipped me to my stomach and tied me to the bed again, face down.

"Goddammit!" I yelled.

"Mari, you're going to learn not to steal from us, one way or the other." He grabbed the sides of my sweatpants and pulled them beneath my bottom.

Whack.

Oh my god. The fuckers were *spanking* me. And my ass burned like it was on fire.

"The fuck! Goddammit, you'd better not lay another hand on me," I screamed.

Christian leaned close to my ear. "You'd better not let your sticky fingers get the better of you again."

Whack.

"Ugh," was all I could grunt as he put more force behind his swing.

Whack.

The pain was taking my breath away. Despite my pride, despite everything I knew, I was quickly reduced to near tears.

"C'mon guys, I got the message," I whispered, thinking they'd stop.

I mean, what did they want? Cry *uncle*?

Whack.

"Please. Please… " I managed.

Whack.

"I… I got the message," I mumbled. "Please stop."

Whack.

Okay, it was clear my pleading was going to get me nowhere, and that I just had to ride out the cruelty they'd decided I deserved. They would pay, and pay dearly for this, but for now I had to find a way to survive.

Whack.

So what I did was close my eyes and take deep, even breaths, like in yoga class. But despite my efforts toward calm, tears continued welling in my eyes, and began to leak onto the mattress beneath me.

I lost track of the number of times they smacked my ass, and couldn't even tell any longer who was doing it, but one strange thing occurred.

I had this funny tingle in my core. Like, um, I was getting turned on.

Oh my god, what a weirdo I was, getting hot from being spanked.

The bedroom door opened, there was some shuffling of footsteps, then the door closed again. Changing of the guards?

I braced myself for another hit.

But instead, this time, a cool palm smoothed the fiery skin of my ass. I jumped, the sensation was so unexpected. While it was nice, in a strange way it also hurt more than the actual spanking.

I sniffled, alerting one of the guys.

This time, Red's voice was in my ear. "Have you had enough for now, Nursey?"

I nodded, my face buried. I didn't want them to know the effect they'd had on me, even though it was pretty goddamn obvious, especially when Red's fingers wandered down the crack of my ass between my legs.

"Damn, Vic, feel how wet our little thief is."

Another hand smoothed over my ass cheeks, then wandered between my legs.

"Is my punishment over?" I croaked.

Someone snickered.

"Oh no, Nursey. Not yet," Red murmured. "Not by a long shot."

Regardless, one of them undid the ties that held me to the bed.

Red and Victor helped me stand, then handed me a big glass of water. Guess they knew I wouldn't be sitting for a while.

"Take off the rest of your clothes."

I must have looked at them with the most pathetic of expressions, because Red sent Victor a look and said, "Take your time."

I wriggled out of my sweatpants, which were already down to my knees. I caught Red admiring his shaving masterpiece of the day before, until I turned my back to them to remove my top.

"Whew. That is one red ass," Victor whistled.

I threw my discarded clothes on the floor, and continued facing away from them. I wasn't going to give them the satisfaction, not right now.

"You can turn around now," Red said.

"Why? What do you want?" I hissed, pissed off.

"You'll be coming downstairs now to start cleaning the house."

Oh. I reached for my clothes on the bed.

But Red blocked my grasp.

"Without clothes."

I whipped around. "What? Clean house? With no clothes on?"

The guys nodded. "Yup."

All right. I could clean naked. I'd hold my head up and do a great job. Make them feel badly for treating me so shitty.

"Fine. Let's go. You kinky motherfuckers."

12

CHRISTIAN

MARI STRUTTED DOWN THE STAIRS, PROUD AS A PEACOCK. I had to hand it to her—even though she was in deep trouble in the little world we four guys shared, she had found a way to retain her dignity. To the extent that she could, anyway.

Shoulders back, head held high, she walked toward Dutch and me, her large breasts swinging delectably.

"You need something cleaned?" she asked, rotating to see us all as Red and Victor settled into their soft leather chairs.

I nodded. "Yeah. The house."

"Fine," she replied, her eyebrow lifting. "Does it matter where I start?"

Fuck if she didn't look like a brunette Lady Godiva

with long curls twisting over her shoulders, her slim waist flowing into curvy hips. They were kind of hips I loved holding, and that made my dick twitch uncontrollably. And that bastard Red had shaved her bare.

Why hadn't I thought of that?

"You can start here in the living room with the dusting. Cleaning supplies are under the kitchen sink," I said.

She walked purposefully to the kitchen, and returned with furniture wax and a dust rag.

"Where are you guys going while I'm cleaning?" she asked.

I glanced at the others, who couldn't take their eyes off her.

Yeah, we weren't going anywhere.

"We're staying right here to watch," I replied. "To… assess your skills."

Well, that must have been the last thing she expected, because she blushed all the way down to the tops of her pretty tits.

"You… you're just gonna watch me clean?"

I pressed my lips together in a little smile and nodded.

Had she really thought she was going to get off that easy? Yeah, she was going to clean, that's what she was there for after all, and as part of her punishment, she was going to do it butt naked.

As one of the guys had pointed out when we

discussed what to do with her, it'd be a lot harder for her to run away without clothes on.

And until she confessed to stealing from us, that's how things were going to be.

She wouldn't last long. I—well, all the guys really— was pretty expert in coercing confessions from people. It wasn't easy to be tough and decisive, but everyone had a breaking point, and we'd surmised that Mari's would be within minutes of forcing her to parade before us with no clothes. Yeah, it was aggressive action, actually riding the line in a lot of ways. But we didn't fuck around, and we weren't going to be fucked around with, either.

To her credit—I should have known she'd be a little tough-ass—she began to hum as she cleared things from every surface, pretending to be perfectly content with her duties, lack of clothing notwithstanding.

She moved furniture, got into corners, and left no artifact unturned as she easily put on one of the fucking hottest shows I'd ever seen a woman perform. And she was barely even trying.

In no time, she realized just how badly she was driving us crazy, and took advantage of it. She started playing with us, bending over to show off her goods and hang her tits in front of us at every turn. When she popped her ass up just a little as she worked over a shelf, I nearly busted a zipper with my cock.

She wanted to dance with the devil?

Game on.

"Mari, could you come over here? I think I see a spot you missed," I said, pointing to the floor right in front of my feet.

"What?" she asked, hands on her sexy hips, squinting at my imaginary dirt. "There's nothing there."

"You gotta get closer. Right there," I said, getting out of my club chair to direct her. "Here, look."

I crouched and put my finger on the floor. "See?"

She crouched too, and leaned close to my finger. "I still don't see anything, Christian."

"Get closer."

She put her face inches from the floor, searching.

"Okay, Mari. Now keep your face down there."

"What?" she said, popping back up.

"Put your head back where it was," I growled, gently guiding her back.

"Why? What for?" she asked.

"Now, keep it there," I said, stepping back.

Well, you would have thought the guys had just won the lottery with the way they were grinning at Mari with her face to the floor and ass in the air, a rag in one hand, the other holding furniture polish.

But what really killed all of us was the gleaming wetness that had started to leak from her pussy and over her swollen lips, with her ass cheeks still bright pink from the spanking.

"You seem kind of turned on, Mari," I said.

She just *humphed*. "What can I say? I turn myself on."

I chuckled and got right next to her ear. "Is that so? I gotta tell you baby," I said softly, "you got me fucking turned on as hell."

"I'll bet," she said, her voice muffled.

"Yeah, you do. In fact, I'm pulling my dick out right now."

She turned to look, but I put my hand on the back of her head, not pressing but firm.

"Stay right where you are," I growled.

She froze in place.

In about two seconds my hard cock was in hand, which I squeezed for my first drop of precum. Then I took a scoop of Mari's wetness, and dragged it down my length, from root to tip and back again. Freaking amazing, and I knew the other guys were just as turned on as I was.

"You know how fucking hot you are, baby, with your ass in the air like that?" I murmured, stroking faster. All I wanted was her. I wanted to fuck her deep and hard, and it took all my control not to give that to her instead of the last of her 'punishment'. That would come later, if she were into it.

She wiggled a bit, and that was all I needed. Five more strokes, and I spurted my seed all over her back in long ropes, covering her in her sticky white.

"Fuck, look what you do to me, baby," I groaned pulling her into my arms where I laid a lush kiss on her beautiful mouth. She kissed me back, and I knew she understood… maybe there'd be more, but I knew in that kiss the truth. She was just as goddamned turned on as I was.

"Dude. They don't call Christian *minute man* for nothin'," Dutch said, laughing.

I flipped him the bird while I kept my arms around Mari. Like he would have lasted any longer?

"Sucks, to be you, brother," I said, pulling our girl to her feet and guiding her up the stairs.

Enough housekeeping for one day.

"I NEED THE BATHROOM," she said dreamily.

"Sure. We need to get you cleaned up."

As soon as we were there, I grabbed a towel and wiped down her back.

"How's that?"

"Good," she said, nodding. "I have to use the bathroom now. You know, to pee."

I held my hands up as if in offering. "Go right ahead."

She looked at me, waiting.

"Privacy, please?"

As if I didn't know what she wanted.

"Right. Prisoners don't get privacy. It's one of the rights you forfeited when you stole from us."

She looked horrified, but nevertheless sat down on the toilet in front of me.

"Really, Christian? You want to watch me pee now?

It wasn't enough to watch me clean house naked and then jerk off all over my back?" She shook her head.

"Hey, I didn't do it because I wanted to. I *had* to. Now, I'll wait for you outside."

She emerged a minute later, and stood in the bathroom doorway, shaken but defiant.

I liked that. She had heart.

I placed my hands on her shoulders and bent to kiss her neck, now a little salty from the workout she'd gotten cleaning. Her mouth found mine, kissing me with unmistakable hunger.

I followed her to the bed, where she sat and opened my pants back up. She slid them down my thighs, and pulled my shirt over my head.

My cock was already hard again, that's how fucking hot she was, and I watched her lower her lips to my swollen head. She licked my rim and slowly worked her way around the sensitive spots, creating a tight suction that nearly blew my fucking mind.

But her hand on my balls was what sealed the deal.

"Lean back," I growled, kicking my jeans off the rest of the way.

But before I dropped them, I grabbed a condom from my pocket.

I pushed her legs open so I could see close up what had been on display in the living room with the other guys watching. But right now, she was all mine. Only mine. Just what I'd wanted since I'd first chatted her up at the truck stop.

She was still soaked in her own cream, and as much as I wanted to fuck her right then, I needed to taste her first.

When I burrowed my tongue in her hole, her bucking hips nearly threw the two of us off the bed. Her cries tore through the room, and I bet through the entire house.

"You like that, baby?" I asked.

"Mmmm. Uh huh," she groaned. "Makes my pussy scream."

But I wasn't through yet. I ran my tongue between her pretty ass cheeks, and then all the way up to her hard clit, which I tongue lashed with a force that had her head banging against her bare mattress, and her hands reaching for something to grab.

I continued my circles on her clit and entered her gushing pussy with my thumb. In seconds, she screamed again, her inner walls tightening. I let her ride it out for a moment, then pulled out and rolled a condom on.

As she tried to catch her breath, I positioned my cock at her opening and plunged deep inside. I held myself there, her eyes locked with mine, her hands gripping my tense arms.

"You good, baby?" I whispered.

"Yeah. I'm good," she answered, running her hands up my arms and to the sides of my face. "Still pissed at you, but good."

I grinned, rocking in and out of her in response.

Balanced on my knees above her, I watched her tits sway from side to side. There was no way I could get enough of this woman who, even though she'd made a grave mistake, had taken her punishment like a trooper.

I leaned forward and sucked hard on her tits, driving until my balls tightened. She was bucking underneath me, taking everything I had and wanting more, milking me as we both vaulted into the abyss. All I could see was white.

Over the blood that was roaring through my ears, I'm pretty sure I heard her calling my name, over and over again.

***

"You are incredible," I said, pulling her to me.

"Mmmm," she murmured, snuggling into my arms. "You too."

"I can't spend the night with you, though, I'm sorry," I said.

She flipped to look at me, hurt in her eyes. "Really? Why?"

Of course she was going to ask that.

"I… I can't. I have night terrors," I admitted. "I can't have anyone in my bed, even when I want. It's dangerous."

"Really? I'm sorry. Does it have to do with… what you guys have been through?"

She was starting to catch on. We hadn't told her much, but she was putting the pieces together and learning the price of doing some of the things we'd done.

"You can't even try?" she asked sweetly, laying her hand on my chest. "I… I could really use it."

Tempting… but even if I *could* spend the night with her, it would royally piss the other guys off. After all, we were punishing her for stealing.

"Nope. Can't do it. In fact, the guys have to lock me into my room every night."

The look of horror on her face didn't feel good, I'll admit. The last thing I wanted was pity. I'd made my career choices, and was prepared to live with the consequences.

"Is there anything—"

I shook my head. "No. But thank you for asking, and in fact, I think it's time to turn in right now."

I kissed her on the forehead and picked my clothes up from the floor. Feeling like shit, I left her there on her bare mattress without a stitch of clothing on, locked her door from the outside, and went to my own room at the far end of the hall.

At least she wasn't tied up any more.

I was getting comfortable with a book, when there was a sharp knock on my door.

"You in there, Christian?" Dutch asked.

"Yup," I called back, turning the page of an old vampire novel. Cheesy as hell, but horror helped me fight off the real terrors in my head sometimes. "Go ahead."

The key to my bedroom door turned from out in the hallway, leaving me alone with my nightmares where I couldn't hurt anyone but myself.

13

MARI

IT TOOK ME ABOUT FIVE MINUTES AFTER THE DOOR closed and thinking about how I came be punished the way I had to realize I'd been set up, and about five minutes and five seconds to realize I'd been set up by that bitch Leeann.

And while my 'punishments,' such as they were, were total bullshit, I vowed to prove my innocence and get my revenge against her at the same time.

'Course I also had to plan a way to return home without being taken out by gangbangers, but first things first.

Who knew my relatively peaceful life of nursing

and hanging out with girlfriends would take on so much unexpected drama?

I wasn't even a drama kind of girl.

Then again, I also wasn't the 'do three hot guys in two days' kind of girl either. But there I was, freshly fucked and furiously naked, locked in my room without even any bed sheets because I'd been wily enough to use them to escape out my second story window. At least they'd not taken my little coverlet away, which I wrapped myself in for a good night's sleep.

On the bright side, as long as I was locked in, I didn't have to do any house cleaning.

When the morning sun woke me, I pulled open the huge French doors, the scene of my earlier crime, and stepped onto the balcony. It was a gorgeous morning in the mountains with a brilliant blue sky and slight pine-scented breeze. Too bad I couldn't get out to enjoy it.

Although I'd certainly enjoyed myself the night before.

And the night before that.

My breath hitched when I recalled the erotic moments of the last few days. Not only had the sex been surprising—hot tubs, outdoor showers, and my after-spanking comedown—but to enjoy the carefully honed strength of my four lethal hosts was the kind of thing that just didn't happen every day.

I mean, sure, I'd dated nice-looking men. But these guys weren't just nice-looking. They were as beautiful and hazardous as exotic racecars. And it was more than just their looks… there was something about them that had me tossing aside all my reservations and doing some crazy shit I'd never considered before.

Yup, my time on Savage Mountain had been a thrill-a-minute. Something I'd never forget, assuming I'd eventually make my way home and remain alive.

I whipped my gaze in the direction of some commotion coming from the front of the house. Because my room, and therefore balcony, faced the back, I couldn't get a read on what was happening.

Was it possible the gang had found me at the cabin? *No. Way.*

The noise moved into the house, leaving my stomach in a sick churn just like the night I realized I'd been followed onto the Greyhound bus. I pressed my ear to my bedroom door and slowly turned the knob to make sure it was still locked—although, if it were locked from the outside, it wouldn't do me a damn bit of good. I looked around for a place to hide—there was a big closet, and all the standard bedroom fare, but not much more—

The doorknob turned in my hand. All the way.

It wasn't locked.

I didn't know whether to be thrilled or terrified. Maybe a bit of each would have been wise.

But how long had it been unlocked? I could have sworn I heard Christian lock it when he left me the night before.

What a dumbass I was to not even have checked it.

I pulled the coverlet tighter around me and opened the door as silently as I could. The latch made an almost-inaudible *click*, and then I was peering through a tiny crack into the hallway.

Free!

Whatever noise had been brought into the house was back out front now, so I eased the door open to pop my head into the hallway. From my vantage point, there was no one around. I tiptoed into the hall and saw all the bedroom doors open, even Christian's. When I peeked inside I could see his bed had been made. There were no other signs of life.

"Hey!" someone hissed.

I whipped in the direction of a stern whisper. Dutch stood at the top of the stairs, scowling at me.

"Get back in your room. Lock the door."

I was so shocked to see him I just stood there for a moment. Then, my legs came to life and I scurried away, locking my door behind me.

But what the hell good would a little bedroom door lock be if someone really wanted to get in my room? I'd wager to say it wouldn't do a goddamn thing to stop someone bound and determined.

Unable to resist my sick curiosity, I pressed my ear back against the door, and when Dutch's footsteps faded, I opened it again.

I didn't know what the hell was going on, but I sure

wasn't going to just sit around like a lamb going to slaughter.

I pulled my own door closed behind me, and darted down to Christian's room.

First, I needed clothes. All my stuff was gone, so I quietly rummaged in his dresser until I found a sweatshirt and pants. They looked ridiculous, but at least I was covered. I rolled up the too-long sleeves and tied the drawstring on the pants tight to keep everything on. Then, I stuffed my coverlet under his bed, and started looking for places to hide. Then maybe, just maybe, I could figure something out.

I didn't know yet what that something was. But I was working on it.

Suddenly I heard the voices, both familiar and strange, that, fortunately, seemed to be staying downstairs.

Until they weren't.

Heavy footsteps bounded up the steps, and my pulse just about pushed my heart into my throat. I glanced around wildly and stepped into Christian's closet, pulling the door partially shut behind me.

Real original. Wasn't that how just about every dumbass female character in a horror movie got herself killed?

Too bad my survivor shows hadn't covered how to protect yourself *inside* a house.

I burrowed into Christian's plaid flannel shirts, doing

all I could to not trip over his collection of boots. I nearly yelped when something sharp dug into the soft bottom of my bare foot, but I stopped myself just in time.

Then, as quickly as the voices came, they left. Someone must have forgotten something in their room.

I could breathe again. I slowly extricated myself from Christian's clothes, and while picking my way out of his closet, noticed a long cupboard on the inside, just above the door.

Funny place for a cupboard.

And because I was a nosy pain in the ass, I pulled the hinged door open to see what it held.

No big surprise.

I was faced with a collection of neatly stacked guns on some sort of rack built into the wall above. I didn't know shit about firearms, but those I was staring at were in several shapes and sizes, and looked scary as hell.

"What are you doing?"

I dropped the cupboard door closed with a loud bang and turned to find Dutch watching me.

I rushed toward him, wringing my hands, hoping for some understanding.

"Dutch, I was just looking for some clothes to wear, then I heard strange voices and thought it might be the gang members after me, so I hid in Christian's closet, and when I was coming out, I saw that cabinet up there."

I strained to look up at him, that's how tall he was, and the width of his shoulders cast a shadow could have blotted out the sun. He gave me a half-smile, showcasing one of his dimples, damn him, and placed a giant hand on my shoulder, which reminded me of our naughty little tryst in the hot tub.

"Slow down. You're gonna hyperventilate," he said. "First off, those gangbangers aren't here. If they were, you'd have nothing to worry about anyways. They couldn't get within five hundred yards of this place without having a really bad fuckin' day."

Sweet relief. Geez, I was tired of being scared. I wanted to get lost in his arms, but was it appropriate since they'd branded me a thief?

"What was all that noise? I was terrified."

Dutch tilted his head. "Don't worry about that. It had nothing to do with you."

"Then why did you tell me to get in my room—"

"There are times when you just have to stay out of the way. Okay?" he asked, eyebrows raised. "It's… complicated."

"Sure. Whatever."

He ran his hand down my back, soothing away my goosebumps. Thank god I was covered up in Christian's oversized clothes, or else I really would have been a mess.

"Do you want to come down for something to eat?" he asked.

I hadn't thought about food since the night before, and I was freaking starving.

"Yes, please!"

I took my customary place at the kitchen counter, keeping an eye out for the horrible Leeann. I'd show everyone who she really was as soon as I had some evidence. I was a patient woman.

Dutch gestured toward the dining table where he and the guys always ate.

Huh?

He must have noticed the confusion on my face, because he clarified. "Come sit over here, at the table."

Was this some weird part of my punishment?

I furrowed my brow, but climbed down from my stool just the same. "Are you sure?"

He smiled, and it transformed his face from handsome to... something else. Something special, and something that twinged inside me. "Yeah. Grab a seat. I'll get you something to eat."

Without another argument, I slipped into one of the heavy wooden dining chairs, and watched him make me a plate in the kitchen.

He delivered me a delicious meal of salad and cold, herbed chicken on the side. I hadn't realized how starving I was for something tasty, and had to stop myself from inhaling the food like a little piggy.

"Dutch, I didn't steal the box—" I started.

But he held his hand up like a *stop* sign. "Let's not talk about that now."

I shrugged. Fine. I'd follow his lead for the moment. But I would prove my innocence eventually.

He folded his hands on the table while I stuffed my face. "What I want to talk about are the guys who are after you. Can you give me any more information?"

Oh *that*. The reason I was in the freaking mountains to begin with.

"Well, my girlfriend invited me to her cousin's… " I said, not stopping until I'd gone through the whole drama, careful to not leave out any detail.

He chuckled. "So you really killed a man?"

Why did he have to say it like that?

"I did, but I didn't mean to," I protested. "It was a total accident. Dutch, I'm a *nurse*. I save people. You know how this feels? I'll have to live with it for the rest of my life."

My appetite was gone. Apparently, homicide will do that to you.

He leaned toward me, over the table. "You know what you will have to live with for the rest of your life? The honor of saving saved your friend from being raped by a piece of shit who didn't deserve any form of mercy. So how 'bout you reframe your thinking there?"

I stared at him without a thing to say.

"You know we guys are former military and now provide private security services, right?" he asked.

"Yeah."

Not sure I wanted to know more than that.

"I know how it is to kill people," Dutch explained.

"But when you focus on the good reason for it, it takes on a different meaning."

I tried to hide the tears welling in my eyes, but it was pointless.

Dutch reached across the table and took my hand.

"What I'm wondering is, why you reacted so strongly to what happened to your friend. Did something like that happen to you, once?"

Oh, fuck. The tears were now flowing.

"Y… yes. H… how did you know, Dutch?" I asked, my voice coming in spasms.

"Mari, I've seen a lot of things and know a bit about human behavior," he said softly. "I knew there was more to the story. There always is."

I looked down at my plate, which was now becoming saturated with my salty tears. I was too embarrassed to look at Dutch, now that he knew my deepest shame.

"Hey. Look at you. You came out on top," he continued quietly. "You didn't let anyone ruin you. You're smart, beautiful—I mean, you're a freaking nurse. You know how guys fantasize about nurses? They're freaking hot."

I looked at him through watery eyes, and couldn't help but burst out laughing.

"That's absurd," I said. "Nurses aren't hot."

He shrugged, and gave me that giant grin.

"Yeah, well mountain men aren't hot either," he said with a laugh.

He had me there.

14

DUTCH

"Hey guys, heading out?" I asked as Christian, Victor, and Red joined Mari and me in the dining room.

"Yup. Heading down the mountain," Victor said, resting a hand on Mari's shoulder.

When he did, she jumped. Couldn't say I blamed her. But she'd do herself a huge favor if she would just own up to how the hell the Persian box got in her room.

"Wh... where are you guys going?" she asked, keeping her eyes on the plate in front of her.

"We're going to town, beautiful. Gotta pick up some

provisions, those sorts of things, ya know," Victor answered, taking a seat next to her at the table.

Setting her fork down, she turned to him, keeping her voice level despite the obvious eagerness she must have felt. "I'd like to go. I need a few things. Clothes, for one," she said, gesturing at the oversized sweats she'd swiped from Christian. "And… womanly things."

Victor shook his head sadly. "No can do, my friend." Then he got up and headed for the door with the other guys.

"But hey," he added, stopping, "I'll pick you up some things. I have good taste, don't worry."

She nodded, somewhat shocked, then looked at me. "Aren't you going, too, Dutch?"

"Nope. Staying here with you. Sorry. You're stuck with me," I said. "Gonna keep the hairy eyeball on you."

I could have sworn her face brightened, but maybe I was flattering myself with wishful thinking.

"Have fun, kiddos," Victor said, pulling the door closed.

I'D KNOWN Victor since we'd met at boot camp, many years ago. It was hot at Fort Benning, Georgia, so hot they used to say that it was owned by the Devil, who rented it out to the Army while he preferred the more comfortable environs of Hell. I'm not sure if it was that bad, but pretty close.

We immediately hit it off, polar opposites as we were. I was serious about making the best impression I could in order to get college scholarships, and Victor's main goal in life was to skate by with the bare minimum of work, and fight off the many girls who were always chasing after him. Despite that, we both shone as the highlights of a 'summer surge' platoon.

Like a lot of those basic training buddies, we eventually fell out of touch. But I was pleasantly surprised when, years later, our paths crossed. I'd become a doctor, paid for by the U.S. government, and Victor was a famous sharp shooter. Well, famous within the dangerous little world we were about to start living in.

Speaking for myself, I'd long since paid back any investment the government had made in me, and I was now ready to benefit from the private sector offers I'd been bombarded with for years. I'd been assigned to head up the medical crew for a dark ops team, working in places on the planet that Uncle Sam preferred not to have actual troops. Dangerous and borderline unethical, but I'd only have to do it six months out of the year, and would be paid more for those months than I'd been in my last three years with the military.

I got my honorable discharge, volunteered at a refugee camp in Uganda for a month, then reported for duty.

I couldn't have been more surprised by my new gig. There were no uniforms, the food was more than decent, and my 'quarters' had a TempurPedic mattress, full air conditioning, and even a PlayStation if I wanted it. If I overlooked the fact that I worked in a room that used to be part of a large warehouse, my new gig was like being in some weird kind of first class military. Only the work was much more dangerous, and depending on whom you asked, illegal.

Victor had been brought in as the outfit's sharp shooter. For five months, it'd been easy living. He and his boys went out to inflict damage, and I spent a lot of my time sitting back, catching workouts in the well-equipped gym in our 'base', and treating an even dozen cases of the clap for the boys who got 'local entertainment'. There were some hairy times during a few patrols I had to pull when they needed a medic with them, but nothing too crazy.

It had been great to reconnect with my friend until shit went south and he became a hostage. I'd always felt guilt-ridden for escaping unscathed. But when he did get out, thanks to our employer's ability to negotiate large ransoms before crushing those who dared to hurt us, we renegotiated our commitments, and escaped to Savage Mountain.

BUT JUST BECAUSE we'd gone through hell and back together, it didn't mean I agreed with everything he did.

Like taunt Mari with his trip to town. There's

teaching discipline, and then there's just being an asshole.

"Would you like to go for a walk?" I asked after we finished eating. "Screw the cleaning for a bit?"

Her face brightened, and she nodded. "Oh my god, that would be great. I'm dying for some fresh air, and to stretch my legs."

She took her plate off the table and turned to me. "But I thought I wasn't supposed to go anywhere. You know, being punished, and all."

"Isn't being stuck with me, wearing those clothes, punishment enough?" I teased.

She smiled, happy to accept some freedom, however limited.

"Let me get my sneakers," she said, her smile dimming a little. "They're about the only thing you and the other goons didn't take away from me."

I couldn't blame her for being irritated.

It was a beautiful day on the mountain and Mari and I walked for about twenty minutes in silence, just listening to the sounds of the wilderness. It was what I loved about hiking. You could be with another person, enjoying yourself, and not have to flap your gums the whole time.

And Mari *got it*. A lot of women would feel they had to fill the silence with chatter.

But not her.

"Here we are," I said, stopping when I reached my target.

She looked around, confused. We were in the middle of a narrow trail with heavy forest on each side. "Where?"

"Watch," I said. "You're gonna love this."

I stepped around the tree we'd been standing under and scurried up some railings I'd nailed into the trunk. With a small tug, a cleverly hidden rope ladder unfurled right in front of us.

Her eyes widened. "What is this, Dutch?" Her gaze followed the ladder to a structure built thirty feet in the air. She craned her neck, shadowing her eyes against the sun. "What the heck is that?"

"That is my treehouse," I said with a grin. "Come on up."

She looked at me like she was crazy. It was a look I was familiar with. Couldn't blame her. The guys thought I was nuts, too. But when you only worked a few months out of the year, you needed to fill your days. And I'd always wanted a treehouse.

"You have a *treehouse*?" she asked, amused. "Is it a magic treehouse?"

"Laugh all you want," I said, grinning. "I am the envy of ten year old boys all around the world."

"Seriously?" she asked, shaking her head. She looked up at it again, and smiled a little. "I guess you would be."

"Let's go," I said, taking her hand and showing her the first step.

She scratched her head and looked around. "I don't

know. You want me to *climb* that thing?" she asked, pointing at the ladder.

"It's completely safe," I assured her. "Each rope is rated to pull a truck, and…" I took the bottom rung of the ladder and secured it to a hidden stake in the ground, which pulled it taut. "Now it's secure. Would you like me to go first?"

I knew the treehouse was eccentric, but nothing about my life was normal, if you thought about it. And part of me really wanted to show Mari this side of my life.

"Yeah. You go. I'll follow," she said.

Well, I'd been up in the treehouse a hundred times, so I made quick work of the ladder, pulling myself up on the structure's platform. I leaned out over the hatch to watch her climb.

"Your turn now. C'mon. You can do it."

She smiled and put her foot on the first rung and then the second. Gaining confidence, she kept going, joining me in the house in seconds.

"This is amazing, Dutch!" she said once she reached the main platform. She did a three hundred sixty degree turn to enjoy the dramatic view over the canyon. "Takes my breath away."

"I thought you might like it," I said, warmed. "I built it up on this hill primarily for the view. Took me weeks to find the right tree."

Christ, she looked hot in her light sheen of sweat from our walk, even though she was wearing Christian's ridiculously large clothes. She turned around again, and smiled. "Thank you."

"You're welcome," I answered, grinning. "Now, can you come over here and kiss me?"

It was the first time I'd seen her look relaxed. With one hand on the treehouse's railing, her bow-like lips twitched in a sly little smile.

Game on.

"Don't you think you're being a little bossy?" she teased.

"Don't you think you'd better not sass me? I mean, it's a great privilege when a guy lets a girl in his tree house."

She put her hands on her hips, and sauntered toward me. "Maybe... sir."

Oh, she knew just what she was doing. When she was finally in front of me, I brushed the hair off her shoulders, and brought my mouth to hers for a lush kiss.

There could be no better setting to share with such a beautiful woman. The sun breathed life into us as leaves brushed across the house's peaked roof, and fresh mountain air drifted through its open sides.

I'd been saving the treehouse to show to a special woman, not sure I'd ever find one, at least not up on Savage Mountain.

And now here she was. Since the moment I'd laid eyes on her at the truck stop and taken down the creep following her, I'd known she was a force to be reckoned with. I'd known men... well, semi-men in my opinion, who liked lifeless yes-women. Sure, those women might have been hot in a physical sense, but they were boring as fuck five minutes into a conversation.

Mari was my kind of girl.

We just had to resolve the matter of the Persian box. But that could wait until later.

I lifted the sweatshirt over her head to get to her perfect tits, and the second my hands were on them, my dick sprang to attention, pressing painfully against the fly of my pants. I brought her nipples to my mouth, my hard sucking causing her to drop her head back with a quiet moan.

In an instance where fate smiles on the world, the woman with the sweetest tits I'd ever seen also loved having them played with. What could be better?

"You like that, baby?" I whispered. "You like these nipples sucked like gumdrops?"

"Yeah. Do it harder," she pleaded.

I gave her just what she wanted, sucking hard and pulling on her nipples until her breath came in short, desperate gasps. I pulled off before she could come just from my mouth.

"Come over here," I said, taking her to the railing. "Isn't it beautiful?"

"Yeah," she said, bending over in anticipation of what came next.

I crouched to pull down her sweats, and had my

own pants at my ankles in seconds. I rolled a condom on and bent her over the railing.

"You ever been fucked outdoors, in a treehouse, baby?"

She shook her head while raising her pretty little backside to open the way for what I was about to give her. "Closest I got was swapping dirty stories with a friend back in high school on a raft in a lake."

I placed one of her feet on the lower rung of the house's railing, and spread her open to set my dick at her opening. "Well now, guess we've checked one off your bucket list."

Her ass was still pink from the previous night's spanking. I had to admit, it turned me on to see it like that. I didn't want her in pain, but that shade of pink… it was almost the same as the inner lips of her pussy, and it had me oozing precum even before I'd gotten inside her.

I inched carefully inside her, giving her time to adjust. Her inner walls gripped me like a goddamn vise, so I moved slowly until she bucked back against me so hard she nearly knocked me to the deck. "God dammit Dutch, stop teasing and fuck me!"

Unbelievable. She still could sass, and was just bossy enough to make it sexy at the same time. She was everything I ever thought a woman should be.

I thrust until I was all the way in. The last half inch slipped in with such a force that my balls slapped against her clit. Just how I liked it.

"Oh, Dutch, fuck me," she cried, slamming her hand on the railing and shaking the whole damn platform.

Fuck, I'd known she was a hot number, but I didn't know to expect this.

Nor, did I think to expect what came next.

"In my ass. I want it in my ass," she begged.

Well, I'll be goddamned. I had a certified dirty girl on my hands. And of course, I was happy to oblige her.

I continued pumping while I wet my thumb and placed it against her pretty little star. With some wiggling, I was inside her tight canal, getting her ready for my hungry dick. The whole time she pushed back, wriggling and clenching around my thumb, opening herself to me.

When she was ready, I withdrew my thumb and pressed against her hole, still not quite ready for me. There was a big difference between my thumb and my dick, so the pressure I applied was slow and gradual.

Mari groaned at the pressure on her back door.

"You good, baby?" I asked. "Like it?"

She nodded, her dark curls flying around her shoulders and down her back.

With my hands on her slim waist, I pulled her toward my cock until my head was all the way inside her, my balls aching with need just from watching her asshole stretch to accommodate me.

"You push back when you're ready, darling."

Who knew how much experience she had in ass play? I wanted to let her take the wheel.

And take the wheel, she did. She leaned back into me slowly but deliberately until I was balls deep inside her, her breath coming in rapid gasps. I pulled back, and started pumping, our bodies clapping together in the intensity of each deep stroke of my cock. Everything faded, the sounds of the forest, the sun on my back, the wind on our skin. All that was left was the woman in front of me, her body joined with mine, and the intense pleasure of our bodies thrashing together.

Mari reached between her legs, rubbing her clit in time to my strokes, and I smiled, holding her hips tighter. "That's it baby... stroke that button. Come all over my thick cock in your tight little ass."

"Oh, oh, oh, fuck me," she screamed, bouncing off my cock as an orgasm shook her from head to toe. Her ring clenched around me, and it was all I could take.

Her climax triggered my own explosion, and I pistoned her until I had nothing left.

Sagging to the deck, I wrapped us in a few of the blankets I kept stored in a weatherproof box, and nestled with her on the wooden floor, my arms wrapped tightly.

I didn't know who was after her for defending her friend, but when I got my hands on them, her problems would be over and theirs would just be starting.

15

MARI

I don't know what came over me.

I mean, I wasn't into anal sex. I'd only ever done it once or twice. Sure, a little teasing, and a tongue? Hey, I wasn't a prude. But something about being up in Dutch's freaking cool-as-shit little hideaway, overlooking the wildness of Savage Mountain, turned me into a Jane to his Tarzan.

Seriously, he did have a Tarzan thing going on, minus the skimpy little loincloth. Towering well over six feet, his wide shoulders could cast shadows as he walked. But at the same time, he moved with a lithe, animal-like grace befitting the lord of the jungle . He was missing a piece of his ear, for fuck's sake, and had been a badass for some 'private security company,' whatever the hell that meant.

I almost didn't care if he was also a doctor. He was still a bad boy, and he sure as hell brought out my bad girl. He wasn't like any of the doctors at the hospital where Luci and I worked, that was for damn sure.

Basically, he was the stuff of dreams—a goddamn hunky badass dude who could take care of business. Take down enemies? Check! Build treehouses? Check! Fuck like a well-hung, dirty pornstar? Double check!

But he was also smart enough to bring home the bacon. And he could cuddle like nobody's business.

My kind of guy. Everyone's kind of guy, actually.

As we snuggled on the floor of his house in the sky that, even though the wind was screaming at our altitude, didn't budge or sway in the slightest, I couldn't quite believe how lucky I'd been to stumble into him. Into *them*. The guys of Savage Mountain. I was out of my element in that place, but in a good way. I was getting busy with four men who all seemed cool with it, and getting some fresh air at the same time.

I had no illusions about it lasting. Hopefully, I'd go back to my former life soon, and my days on the mountain would fade to a sexy memory.

But for now, I was in a freaking treehouse with a hunky man of epic proportions. In fact, the treehouse was probably more solid than the freaking house he and his gang had down on the ground.

"How'd you bring all your materials up here?" I

asked, looking around to see an easy chair and some well-organized bookshelves. "And the furnishings, too?"

Seriously, he pretty much had the place outfitted like a small, personal library. "And what do you do when it rains?"

He kissed the top of my head, which I fucking loved, and laughed.

"Jesus, I'm gonna start calling you Question Girl."

I nudged him, chuckling. Guys like him needed to be reminded who's boss. "You do, and I won't stop," I said.

"I brought everything here on a huge cart we use for… moving things. Then shimmied them up using a pulley," he said, pointing towards a branch overhead that was thick enough to have a pulley attached to it. "It really wasn't a big deal."

Not a big deal for *him*, maybe.

"Okay, how did you get that hulking easy chair up here?" I asked. Seriously, the thing had to weigh more than I did.

"Took it apart, lashed it together, and then hauled it up," he said. "Then reassembled it."

Well, I'll be damned. The guy was a one-man Swiss Army knife.

"And when bad weather comes, I have plastic tarps attached at the roofline that roll down and attach to the walls. It's cool to be here in a storm. It's like being in a rainforest."

Cripes, I really did have my very own Tarzan.

"Do you have a rope you can swing from?" I asked, turning to face him. "Or a zipline?"

"Very funny," he said, pushing me down for another juicy kiss. "But if you want, I do have a long, stiff piece of cable for you to slide up and down on."

Just as things started to get heated again, we were interrupted by a loud squawk.

I bolted upright, my fright nearly shoving him off of me.

"Oh my god. What was that?" I looked around frantically. I knew *Jurassic Park* was just a movie, but the jungle scenes had lingered in my mind for years.

He groaned and leaned over for his pants. "It's the guys. Looking for me."

"The guys?"

He nodded. "We use bird calls, they carry well in the woods up here."

I nodded, then shook my head. "Cripes, have we been away for that long? I thought they were going to be gone all day."

He looked at me with a contented smile. "They have been gone all day, and so have we, pretty much. You dozed off for a bit. Guess I wore you out?"

Good lord, he did. I was going to be walking funny for days… and loving every second of it. "What did you do while I was sleeping?"

He looked around sheepishly. "Well, I watched you for a while. Then I read."

I pulled the blanket to cover myself. He watched me? Was that creepy? Or sweet?

He pulled a walkie-talkie out of his pants pocket. "Hey guys."

There was a lot of crackling, followed by, "Dutch? Where are you? And where is Mari?"

He rolled his eyes, and spoke into the tiny instrument. "I'm in the treehouse. She's with me."

"With you?"

He looked at me, grinning. "What did you think? We took off for Vegas or something?"

The crackling came back on. "Roger that. See you later."

He tossed the walkie-talkie to the floor.

"So," Dutch said, propping himself up on one arm. "I think we may be able to take care of your little problem at home—the one with the gang."

"Really? How?" I asked.

EVEN THOUGH THE guys still seemed to believe I was a thief, they nevertheless wanted to help me with the creeps who were after me. And they'd gotten me new clothes including some utilitarian but comfy panties and a couple bras.

It kind of made up for the spanking. And other stuff. Not all of it, but I was willing to give them a second chance.

The spanking had been sort of hot, anyway. I mean, it was literally hot—my ass was still sore from the burning smacks I'd gotten—but in a very taboo way it had also turned me on. Ceding power, even involuntarily, to these alpha gods was heady as hell. I'd never been into the spanking thing before, aside from messing around, but it was strangely intimate.

As if they'd done it with a certain amount of care.

Ugh. Such crazy talk. You don't whip a woman's ass because you like her.

Or did you? I'd heard about the practice of power exchange and now I wanted to learn more. I'd have to see if they had any books on the matter. They had books on every other freaking topic.

Including gardening. Lots of gardening books. Which I'd begun paying attention to once I'd noticed the bitch Leeann bringing fresh produce into the house. In an attempt to locate where she'd come from with her basketful of fresh-picked vegetables—I didn't bother to ask her, what would be the point?—I'd followed a short path through the woods that led to a huge, sunny clearing that could provide enough food for a small city.

They grew all the basics—lettuce, green peppers, tomatoes—but also cooler stuff like artichokes, garlic, and asparagus. There was even one long row of straw-berry plants.

It was beautiful.

I pulled a pepper off its vine, and bit into it like it

was an apple. The darn thing was still warm from the sun.

"Hey, do you think that stuff is free?" boomed a voice behind me.

"Shit!" I screamed, dropping my delicious pepper into the dirt.

Dammit. The pepper had been really tasty.

I spun around to face the handsome Victor, my smooth and suave sniper. If James Bond had been a mountain man, he would have looked just like him with his perfectly trimmed beard, and clothes that looked like he'd walked out of a Ralph Lauren ad.

I mean, I think he *ironed* his plaid flannel shirts.

That was some weird shit.

"Oh hi, Vic." I smiled sweetly. No one had told me I could leave the house, but then they hadn't told me I *couldn't*, either.

I braced myself for a scolding from the resident bad boy. Or even worse.

Why did that excite me?

But he placed his hand on my shoulder and smiled. That, coupled with the warmth of the sun and the smell of good garden dirt, sent a woozy flash of happiness over me, the likes of which I'd not experienced in a long time.

Well, not since I was up in Dutch's treehouse. But still.

"If you're gonna eat the vegetables, you gotta help grow 'em," he said. "I'll show you what to do."

Music to my ears. A job to do, in the beautiful outdoors. What was not to like?

Tingles continued to run down my spine where his hand rested on me.

"I'd love to help. I don't know anything about gardening, though. So if you could give me some pointers, that would be great."

He removed his baseball cap, and set it on my head. "Here. We can't have you sunburned."

Cripes. I hadn't thought about sunscreen. But then, I hadn't known I would be put to work in the garden, either. "Thanks."

He put his hands on his hips, pleased to have an assistant. Or maybe he just wanted company? "Okay, let's start with picking what's ripe. Once we get that off the vine, we'll remove dead foliage and pull any weeds."

I followed him to a shed on the edge of the clearing, where he handed me what looked like a big laundry basket.

"You can tell when stuff is ripe, right?" he asked.

"Um, I think so. I mean it just looks ready to eat."

He chuckled. "Good enough. Start with these rows, and pick what you might want to eat. Not too much, just enough for the house."

I crouched in the little drainage dip between the rows of peppers and cucumbers and got a few of each into my basket, imagining a wonderful salad… right up until my heart stopped at what I saw.

Holy fuck.

My scream came from somewhere primal, tearing through my throat before I even knew what I was doing. The reason was simple... a goddamn snake slithered across the dirt not two inches from my foot.

"What's wrong? What's wrong?" Victor asked, scanning the perimeter of the clearing, his hand resting on his hip.

Did he have a gun in his pants?

For god's sake, where *was* I?

I'd backed away from the snake so quickly I'd stumbled and fallen ass-first on top of a strawberry bush. The little berries didn't stand a chance and their juices oozed through the fabric of my new shorts and down the backs of my legs.

Seeing no issues on the horizon, Victor moved his hand from his hip. "What the hell was that?"

I scrambled to my feet, and tore ass back to the house.

"Snake!" I called over my shoulder, not pausing to see if he'd heard me.

"YOU KNOW, garden snakes are completely harmless," Red chuckled when I told him my tale of horror. He'd found me sitting on the front steps, concerned about how many other snakes might be out there. "They actually help keep the garden clear of rodents."

"I guess. It just freaked me out."

He nodded, a lock of his red hair bouncing off his forehead. God was having a good day when he made this man, that was for damn sure. Hottest ginger I'd ever seen in my life. He seriously put Prince Harry to shame.

"But I didn't know if it was a rattler or something. You know?"

"We don't have them around here, don't worry. Hey, Dutch told me you guys visited the treehouse. It's really something, isn't it?" he asked.

Thoughts of the snake faded.

"Yes, it was so cute. Such an awesome getaway."

Red leaned closer to me on the front steps where I'd settled. I couldn't sit anywhere in the house with my strawberry-stained behind.

"It is nice, isn't it?" he asked, running a finger down the front of my shirt. I smiled, biting my lip as he slipped a hand inside it.

"I don't think you're talking about the treehouse any more."

Even with a busted nose he was stunning, and the sleeve tattoos on his fair skin were the perfect bad boy contrast to his oh-so-innocent freckles and hair. My nipples sprang into action as he stroked them, as did the bulge in the front of his jeans.

Tilting his head, he looked at me. "I gotta tell you, Mari. You have the most distracting breasts in the world. Especially when you're not wearing a bra."

Oops. Busted. I'd not thought anyone was around

when I'd gone out wandering. To be honest, I'd gotten lazy in the underwear department. I mean, they'd gotten me two bras when they'd gone to town. Added to the one I had when I arrived, I had to make them last.

Right?

So I'd taken to traipsing around with my 32D's free and unfettered. Yeah, I was a little big to go braless, but the girls were still perky, so what was the harm?

Actually, the harm was that I was driving poor Red crazy.

He stood. "Will you come with me?" he asked, taking my hand. "First we need to get that strawberry goo off you."

He started walking before I could protest, but since he had a grip on my hand, I didn't have much choice except to follow. Unless I wanted to be dragged like a cavewoman.

A naughty voice in my mind whispered, *Actually, that might be something fun to try...*

In the kitchen, he took a rag and wiped down my backside like I was a dirty little kid, except that he lingered on the roundest part of my ass.

Uh-huh. "Careful mister, or else I'll make you lick that goo off of me."

Red chuckled, his voice raspy. "What do you think I'm planning on? I just was getting the mud off."

Taking my hand again, I followed him to a part of the house I'd discovered only a couple days before. No one had ever been polite enough to give me a formal tour of the house. So, I'd taken it upon myself to check out the place, unsure of whether or not I was breaking the rules of my semi-imprisonment. Or house arrest. Or whatever it was.

"Hey are you still mad at me about that silver box, which, by the way, I did not steal?" I asked.

Turning his eyes to me, he said, "Can we talk about that later, please?"

I sighed. Was I ever going to get a chance to prove myself on that subject?

We entered the library, a solemn high-ceilinged room that smelled of whisky and crackled leather, where he settled me on a luxurious overstuffed velvet sofa. Leaning me forward just enough to pull my shirt over my head, he discarded my top, and then wiggled his cargo pants down to his ankles, impatiently yanking a foot out of one side.

I was topless, he was bottomless. I could sort of see where this was going…

He palmed his long, thick cock, and stared hungrily at my bare chest.

So to further tantalize him—I mean, why not?—I cupped my breasts as an offering while thumbing my hard nipples. I knew a man who wanted a tit job when I saw one.

When a primal groan built in his throat, I knew my move had had the desired effect.

"You like what you see, baby?" I asked in a small

voice. "You want to rub that thick cock between my breasts?"

"*Fucking A,*" he mumbled, stepping toward me until he was standing against the front of the sofa.

"Get on your knees and bring those tits here," he growled.

I kneeled on the edge of the sofa as he demanded, which brought my chest to the same height as his swinging erection.

Perfect.

I pressed my tits around the hard, warm shaft of his cock, and he placed his huge palms on my shoulders.

"Keep them together for me, baby," Red rumbled. "Hold them tight. I wanna fuck your tits."

I nodded, licking my lips as I massaged my breasts around his shaft, knowing what it would do to him. I wanted to create the perfect tight but soft little channel for him. In just a couple thrusts, his precum combined with my spit made everything nice and slippery.

As he tit fucked me, I looked up at him, our gazes locked as his cock slipped in and out of my heavy breasts.

I couldn't look away from his light blue eyes, which on the surface seemed expressionless, but were telling me something regardless. We were connected and I was able to give him something he took immense pleasure in. How powerful that felt, and even more so when I arched my back to increase the friction against his rock-hard dick.

"Red?"

"Yeah, baby?" he groaned, speeding up.

"I want you to cum all over me. Make me your dirty little slut," I whispered, opening my mouth for his seed. He loved it, and groaning my name, thrust one more time. I watched with pleasure as his eyes fluttered closed and a smile crossed his face.

The first spurt landed right in my mouth, and the rest on my neck and chest, covering me. I arrived on Savage Mountain thinking I was normal, but hells bells, look at me now.

"All right," Red said, laying me back on the sofa, "I believe you deserve a little… reward. And I haven't tasted those strawberries yet."

For once, I was more than happy to obey without question.

16

VICTOR

It had been a couple days since Mari's punishment, and I couldn't believe I still needed to keep an eye on the woman. She was just insatiably curious.

"What are you doing?" I demanded.

Her head whipped around, dark curls bouncing off her shoulders and neck. She was wearing her usual short shorts, hiking boots, and today a cropped T-shirt that showed off the sexy little dimples in her low back right above her waistband. She looked like what Camping Barbie might look like. But better, of course, because her curves were all real.

"Oh hi, Vic." She stepped out from behind the tree where she'd been hiding. Or spying. Or something. She batted her eyes at me, and damn if it didn't make me want to go easier on her. It should be against the law for a woman to be that naturally astute, but I was starting to suspect the laws of nature were on her side.

Christian and Red were far ahead of me on the trail when I found her hiding behind a tree. Cripes, she was sneaky. She gestured to the guys up ahead, who hadn't seen her hiding. "I wanted to be alone. Didn't feel like talking. So I ducked back here when they walked by."

She was such a bad liar. There were plenty of places she could have found privacy.

"Well, now you're busted."

And, she didn't look like she gave a damn.

"How so?" she asked.

"This is the one trail we asked you to stay off."

"What's the big deal?" she asked, looking around. "It's a trail like any other trail around here."

If she hadn't become a nurse, she would have made an excellent lawyer. Why did she have to be such a pain in the ass? A beautiful pain in the ass, but still. "Mari—"

"Fine," she said, crossing her arms over her chest, "I wanted to know where it went. You guys don't tell me anything, you won't even talk about the box I didn't steal. You all have serious communication issues."

She did not just say that, did she?

I grabbed her by the arm. I knew I shouldn't, but she just pushed my buttons so badly, she had me trembling on the edge of control all too often.

"We talk about what we need to talk about," I

growled, keeping my voice low. "The reason we don't discuss a lot of things with *you* is that you don't need to know them. Because there's shit in our lives that we can't trust you with. Do you get it?"

She shrugged like the brat that she was. "So important enough to fuck around with, but not enough to share the truth with. Way to make a girl feel good, Vic," she said defiantly.

I could see I'd hurt her, but it was for her own good. "Believe me, Mari, it's best that you know as little as possible."

She tried to struggle out of my grip, but of course she couldn't. Finally she sighed and jerked her chin down the trail.

"Well, what's that noise in the distance? Can you at least tell me that?"

Pounding footsteps grew closer, momentarily interrupting our encounter.

We turned to find Leeann charging toward us, an M16 slung over her back, looking angry at the world. Just like she always did, actually.

"What the hell is *she* doing here?" Leeann hissed, looking Mari up and down with abject disgust.

Mari responded in kind, the two of them practically alley cats by that point. "What the hell are *you* doing with that big gun?" she asked, instinctively stepping back. "What's with this place and all your damn guns, Vic?"

Leeann rolled her eyes. "It's a rifle, not a gun. Learn

your fuckin' terminology. And it's none of your business."

Leeann then turned to me. "You're late. We're waiting for you."

Cripes. This was just going to create a fucking hour's worth of fresh questions. "Can you get things started, maybe just some target practice?"

Leeann popped to attention and nodded. "Roger that."

She turned on her heel and headed in the direction from where she came. Meanwhile, I turned my attention back to my girl, Mari.

Shit. Did I just say *my girl*? Trouble.

She looked at me with a frown. "*Now* are you going to tell me what's going on?"

Shit. The other guys were going to kill me.

Especially Dutch.

My old battle buddy did not like when I deviated from the plan—whatever that plan might be.

That's why I was so surprised the night he'd shown up with Mari, a beautiful damsel in distress. A wet dream for nearly any man, but for him it was disruptive and dangerous. But I guess when you are an excellent doctor like he was, you learn to follow protocol.

Me, not so much. And it was time to break the rules yet again.

AFTER HIGH SCHOOL, I'd bounced around from one shit job to another, so I wasn't all that surprised when my dad told me shape up or ship the fuck out. I couldn't blame the man, I mean I stunk up his house with pot smoke and the endless round of chicks I brought home to fuck.

I wouldn't have wanted me around, either.

I couch surfed for a while, but that didn't last long. You run out of friends quick when you live like that.

So, one day as I was getting gas for my piece of shit car, wondering if I should show up for my shift at the pizza shop, I spotted an Army recruiting station. Figuring it couldn't hurt and might get my father off my ass for a bit, I walked over. Those fools took me in, and boy, was I lucky they did. I was going nowhere fast.

By some weird twist of fate, I thrived in the Army. I mean, who knew? I wasn't the best-behaved recruit, not by a long shot, but I figured shit out and learned a lot. A string of perfect scores at the range got me into Sniper School, if just by the skin of my teeth because of my rebellious behavior.

As soon as I touched one of those sniper rifles though, everything clicked for me. And somehow, I graduated *number one*.

And after a hiatus where Dutch had gotten his commission and went to med school, we reconnected and were working together again, this time outside of the confines of the Army. And we had a lot of fun, stuff that wouldn't have flown in the Army with him being an officer and me enlisted.

I knew he blamed himself for my ending up a hostage, but shit like that happens when you do the work we did. Unfortunately, proof of that awful time lived on my back in the form of hideous scars, so neither of us could really get away from it.

So we came to Savage Mountain.

"ALL RIGHT. LET'S GO," I said to Mari, setting out on the trail Leeann had disappeared down. "You've already seen this much."

She was silent, hustling to keep up with me, and most likely a little nervous about what lay before her. But when we reached our destination, her reaction was one more of relief than anything else.

"Oh, I see! You have a school," she said, looking at the three buildings and open fields before her. "What kind? Outdoorsmanship?"

"I guess you could say it's a school," I reply. "We call it a 'training center'.

"Ah. A training center for people like you guys."

Yes. She was getting it.

"You're starting to get the idea. We deal with recruits here."

"Recruits?"

I chuckled. "They're not raw, for the most part, so there are no drill sergeants around."

Suddenly Mari turned her head. "What's that noise?" she asked as the familiar popping reached my ears. It was surprising to a lot of people how soft that sound was when you were more than fifty or a hundred meters away.

"Firing range. Want to see it?"

She nodded in excitement. Not the reaction I'd expected, but that was okay.

She followed me across our little campus and her eyes widened at the shooting activity. "Wow. It's all dudes. Well, except for Leeann over there," she said when we got to the line, pointing. "Why is there only one woman?"

"Well, the company we work for selects the recruits. So far, they've only sent men. But Leeann was our cook and saw what we were doing, and asked to be trained. She's actually done really well."

Why was I standing there talking about work on this gorgeous day with a beautiful woman? I wanted to be somewhere alone with her, where I could remove her clothes.

"Oh, I get it," she said. "That's why Leeann hates me. She's used to being the only woman."

I nodded. "Don't take it personally. She was the same with our old cleaning lady."

Mari's gaze snapped in my direction. "So I'm your *cleaning lady,* huh?"

Oh Christ. Here we go.

"Well, that was what you were hired for," I pointed out. "But the only time I've seen you clean so far was when you were dusting the living room. Naked."

I loved how she'd handled that. Another person might have crumbled under the humiliating pressure. But not Mari. She kept her head up and somehow managed to be more beautiful and sexy than ever. "I've cleaned a few more things than that."

I had to hand it to her, she'd cleaned my cock very, very well. And she wasn't going to be shamed by it.

"You want to learn to shoot?" I asked her.

She turned to me, eyes wide open and grinning. "Could I?"

"Yeah," I said, laughing. "But not right now. There are people on the range. We have to remain… professional. And you're not dressed for it."

Disappointment washed over her face. "I guess."

"But I'll show you around. Let's go."

We walked up to the largest building on our small campus, an innocuous-looking structure built to blend into its mountain top surroundings. But the interior was anything but typical.

Mari looked around the classroom outfitted like a fancy boardroom with a huge oak conference table and leather chairs.

"Okay, now what is *that* noise?"

Ah. The thumping next door. Unavoidable, considering what was going on.

"That's the martial arts studio. Dutch is in there with a lesson."

Her mouth dropped open. "Dutch teaches martial arts?"

"Yeah," I reply with a chuckle. "We each have our own specialty. Christian does the classroom teaching, strategy and so forth. You'd be surprised at the amount of bookwork we make our people do. Red works with our partners who put together the teams for the missions. I, obviously, teach firearms usage. And there are a bunch of minor specialties thrown in as well."

I pointed out a smaller building in the center. "That's where the kitchen and dining room is. As part of their training, every recruit learns to prepare their own food. They'll go on most jobs together, so they have to learn to work as a team in every aspect of their lives."

She shook her head in amazement. "Holy crap. This is amazing. I can't believe you guys have this whole thing going on. What if someone found out about it that you didn't want to? What would the story be?"

"We just say we're an outdoor survival skills center. It's simple," I said. "We've actually had it happen from time to time, lost hikers, a ranger since we border a national park, stuff like that. But in the time we've been here, I can say that it's a total of less than half a dozen people who have stumbled upon us."

"Well, I guess the guys who were after me would

never find anybody up here," she said with satisfaction. "This is about the safest place on Earth, isn't it?"

She was right.

"It's highly unlikely that they would, but if they did, they wouldn't stand a chance against us," I assured her. "No one would really. The elite training we've been through is unmatched anywhere in the world. It's how we came to run this place. We're very selective, and only accept a small percentage of applicants."

"Geez," she said. "A whole world I was unaware existed."

"Yeah, not many know about people like us," I confirm. "We do our work in the dark, behind the scenes. But our work impacts people the world over."

Next, I took her to see the barracks, where everyone had their own simple but private room and bathroom.

"Reminds me of a hotel," she laughed. "You should call it Motel 9 Millimeter."

I laughed. "Good one. Let's go up on the roof. C'mon."

This was what I'd been waiting for.

While the accommodations we provided the trainees were simple, the men weren't expected to live like complete Spartans. The building's roof was filled with lush plantings and comfy outdoor seating, along with a barbecue, table tennis, and lap pool.

"It's gorgeous," Mari breathed, taking in the view of the treetops below.

I led her over to the lounge chairs. "You know what else is gorgeous?"

She rolled her eyes. Couldn't say I blamed her.

"I know that was corny. But I meant it. Look at you."

I ran my fingers through her long dark hair, and leaned to place a kiss on her shoulder, warmed from the afternoon sun. And she smelled so good. Just plain, clean girl.

"I'm glad you joined our little family, Mari. I like having you here."

She looked at me with sarcasm. "Even though you guys are convinced I'm a thief?"

I looked down for a moment. "You got me, there."

Time to change the subject. I leaned her back. "And now I'd like to taste you."

A smile spread across her face. She pulled me to her, placing her delicious lips on mine, sighing as we fell together. While we kissed, I unbuttoned the khaki shorts I'd personally chosen for her when I'd gone to town, and shimmied them down her hips.

I pushed her legs open to either side of the lounge chair to see her gorgeous bare pussy, lips swollen in anticipation of my touch, her wetness glistening in the sun.

"Vic," Mari whispered.

"Yeah, baby?" I asked, looking up at her.

She gestured with her chin.

"There's someone over there, and I think they're watching us."

———

17

MARI

I PULLED MY KNEES UP TO MY CHEST, COMPLETELY creeped out, and covered my body as Victor scanned the rooftop deck.

He looked around, his brow furrowing after a moment. "I don't see anybody. What are you talking about?"

"Those plants over there were rustling," I replied, pointing as best I could. "I think someone was hiding behind them. Can you go check?"

He frowned, obviously not happy about our tryst being delayed. He got up and crossed the deck, moving plants and furniture, and even checking the stairs.

After a few moments he returned, shrugging. "I

didn't see anyone. But this time I locked the door so we have the place to ourselves."

Maybe I'd just imagined it. I mean, who would watch us, anyway? Well, Red, Dutch, or Christian might, but they didn't strike me as the kind to just watch. They'd join in.

"Well, where are all the recruits? Could it have been one of them?" I asked, wanting to suggest it was that freak Leeann. But I held my tongue for the time being. I'd expose her in due time.

He shook his head slowly. "They're all at their training stations. At least they're supposed to be." He ran his fingers through his perfect beard. "Plus, I don't know who would even attempt a Peeping Tom act. One little misstep, and you're thrown out of the program. Our line of work encourages independent thinkers, but we can't and don't let that fly here. You'd have to be an idiot to risk so much just to watch some people get it on. Especially when you can get it on the internet for free."

I looked around, creeped out. It made sense. Who'd bother to spy, especially when your smartphone could give you better? But on the other hand, I had to pay attention to the goosebumps that were making me shiver in the warm sun.

My reaction did not go unnoticed by Victor, who rubbed his hands up and down my arms to warm me up.

He stood, and lifted me to my feet. "I have an idea to help you out."

"What's that?" I asked.

He whipped his shirt over his head and dropped his pants to the ground, kicking both items aside, leaving him in just his boxers and looking sexy as fuck despite my worries.

"The pool is heated. Let's go for a swim." He extended his hand, and I took it, craning my neck to look behind him. The pool did look pretty darn nice. And the thought of warming up sounded delicious.

"Sure. Why not?" I grabbed his hand and we ran for the water, where he made a giant cannon ball, splashing water out of the pool.

I guess that fit with his wild man personality. And I was right behind him, determined to wash away any fears.

I held on to his back as he swam around the pool. And now that I was warmed up and relaxed, I deeply wanted to pick up where we'd left off before I'd thought I'd seen a gatecrasher.

"Hey. Come over here," I beckoned, swimming toward a corner of the pool.

He surged out of the water like a breaching whale and dove back under, swimming the entire way under the surface and beating my slowpoke breaststroke.

I guess these guys really were world-class athletes.

I wrapped my legs around him as he pressed me back against the pool wall, our lips meeting in a kiss that left me shaking. I lightly ran my fingers over the ropey scars on his back while his hands wandered to my ass. Cupping it, he pulled me tight against him.

"You feel good, baby," he said in my ear as he ground between my spread legs. "Much better than the water."

From my ass, his fingers wandered further, until they were pressing against my pussy lips, gently prying them open and finding my excited wetness. Beneath where I had my legs wrapped around his waist, his hard dick slipped out of his boxers to press against me.

"I want you, Vic," I whispered. "I want to feel you."

"Yeah? Baby wants some dick?" he teased.

More than that, so much more. But I'd take what I could. I pushed out my lower lip in a pout. "Please?"

He turned me around, bending me forward over the edge of the pool, and holding my hips, said, "Guide me baby."

I reached between my legs and held him, slippery from the water, at my wet opening, slowly pushing my hips back until he was inside. He stretched me open, filling me up, and sending electricity crackling through my body.

"Fuuuuuck," he groaned once inside. "I can't get enough of you."

He fucked me slowly, seating himself deeply with each stroke. I reached for his balls while feeling him slide in and out.

"You want more?" Vic asked, and I nodded. In that

moment, I wanted everything, and I would let this man have all of me to get it.

He sped up, water sloshing around us, supporting my weight as his cock set my nerves on fire. My clit throbbed with pleasure as the thick ridge of his dick ground against me.

The eruption started low in my belly, fanning out like a slow moving flame, until it left my breasts tingling. My head began to involuntarily buck, and I moved my hands to the edge of the pool for purchase, and to push back on his hard dick.

"God baby, I'm gonna come, fuck…" I gasped, clenching around him.

In a quick motion, he pulled out and stood, exploding on my back in warm streams of cum.

He rested for a moment, and when he caught his breath, hoisted himself out of the pool. I rested my head on the deck, overwhelmed by everything, just sighing happily as my body trembled with after effects.

"Hold on. I'll get you a towel."

Guess they didn't want the pool water full of sperm. Not that I could blame them.

As soon as we were dry, we slowly put ourselves back together, stopping for several kisses. It was more tender, more… soulful than before.

"We should head back. Leeann will be getting dinner on the table," he said.

"Yeah?" I asked, shaking my head. "Well, I'll be lucky if she doesn't put arsenic in mine."

WITH THE SUN dipping behind the trees, the walk back to the cabin was especially magical, with just enough light on the trail to see.

"Hey, Vic," I said, my mind coming around to the emotional swell growing inside me, "do you really think I took that box? I need to ask you that. For... reasons."

"I no longer think you took it," Vic admitted. "But I'm not sure about the rest of the guys."

Idiots.

"Well, it's really frustrating to be accused of something I didn't do."

He took my hand in his large palm, sending tingles all over me again, and looked at me with those penetrating eyes. Eyes that could see far and see sharply, looked deeply into me, and really saw me.

"I know," he said, stroking my cheek with the backs of his fingers. "Let me talk to everyone."

I'd been with each guy since arriving on the mountain, and each encounter was better than the one before it. Thank god I hadn't been asked or forced to choose one out of the four, or else I'd be screwed.

Well, in a different way.

"Hey, when you guys going into town again?" I asked.

I could see the cabin in the clearing up ahead.

"Soon, I think."

"Oh good. I'm dying to go."

He stopped short in front of me. "Mari, you won't be able to go."

Wait. Did he just say what I thought he did?

"You're joking, right?" I laughed. "Or am I still everybody's prisoner?"

Victor's bearded face tightened. "Not exactly. It's just that since you now know what goes on up here, we have to put some precautions in place."

I took my hand out of his. Enough with the bullshit.

"Precautions? What does that mean?" I asked.

"We need to get you armed, and teach you to fire weapons," he said. "You have to learn how to protect yourself. By associating with us, you could end up the target of some of the not very nice folks from our past."

I burst out laughing, but forced myself to stop when I saw the solemn look on his face.

"You're serious, aren't you?" I asked, and he nodded, slowly. "Okay. Sorry I laughed. But Vic, I can't stay here forever, I've got to get back to my nursing job."

We entered the cabin, where everyone was at the dinner table, and Leeann was busy slamming pots around. Say what you want about the woman, but she sure as hell could cook. She was carving some sort of huge bird, and there were enough side dishes on the table to feed an army.

Guess she *was* feeding an army, actually.

They'd better enjoy her cooking while they could because once I exposed her for what she really was, she'd be out on her ass. But what if they then asked me to cook?

I took my usual spot at the counter, and tried to think about what Victor said. I needed to change my life.

"Come join us, Mari," Victor said.

Oh my. Invited to the grown ups' table.

I slipped into a chair at the head of the table. "Thanks. I appreciate it."

"Guys, when Mari and I were walking back from the training center just now—"

"You took her to the training center?" Christian asked. "I thought we agreed we wouldn't do that. At least not yet."

Victor held his hands up like a stop sign. "You are right. We did decide that. But… " he glanced at me, "she managed to find it on her own."

Christian slammed his hand on the dining table, looking defeated. "Son of a… "

I wasn't sure whether I should say anything, so I kept my mouth shut for once.

Victor continued. "What I was saying was that Mari asked about getting back to her nursing job."

Okay, there was something to that, because the guys all looked from one to the other, avoiding my eyes.

Time to chime in.

"Um, anyone care to tell me what's going on? Do you all know something about my future that I don't?"

Dutch cleared his throat as Leeann slammed our

plates down in front of us. "We were thinking of hiring you here… long term."

Crash.

Something had been dropped in the kitchen. What a surprise.

"Leeann, everything okay over there?" Dutch asked.

She responded with a grunt, which said plenty despite the lack of words.

Everyone turned back to me.

"We can pay you to stay here and work as our staff nurse."

I burst out laughing. I couldn't help myself.

"Seriously? I have a good job at home—"

"We can pay you more. A lot more," Red chimed in. "And it's a lot better than being the… maid."

I looked around the table. "Guys, I'd only thought of Savage Mountain as a temporary place to stay while I figured out what to do about my problems at home."

Christian leaned his elbow on the table and put his hands together. "We have a physician, as you know," he said, gesturing toward Dutch. "But we could really use additional medical expertise. An extra set of hands for the times Dutch is… unavailable."

"Would you just think about it? No need to decide now," Victor added.

So they'd been planning this conversation…

"But guys, I'm basically imprisoned here. You won't even let me go to town."

Christian waved his hands and shook his head.

"That's temporary," he assured me. "Knowing Vic, he's told you a bit of what you need to know, for your own safety. And in the meantime, tell us what you desire. We'll get you anything you want."

An intriguing offer… but what I wanted most was freedom, and a clear exoneration for a theft I didn't commit.

NEXT DAY, with time on my hands that I didn't know what to do with—*maybe I should take the guys up on their job offer*—I wandered back to the training center to see what was going on. I still wasn't sure if I was even supposed to be going over there, but until they explicitly told me to stay away, I was making myself at home.

Aside from the sounds of target practice from the range, the place was quiet. However, I did hear one voice from inside the classroom building. I walked toward it, and as I got closer, I realized it was Red. I was about to push his office door open to say hi, when I heard some fragments of his conversation that told me that I'd better not.

"Yeah, I heard you the first time," he growled. "I get that you want power over the mineral deposits so you can control the finances, but we're warriors, not fucking magicians. This shit is serious and it's going to take some time."

I heard a muffled voice responding to him, and guessed they were Skyping or something like that.

"Okay, okay," he said. "Payment will be sent through a wired account, offshore. If we decide to take this job, I'll send you the forwarding details."

Shit. I knew I shouldn't have been listening, but the international intrigue was just so exciting. Way more than being a freaking nurse.

What followed was a bunch of *yes* and *no* answers, and more muffled conversation from whomever Red was speaking with.

"Yeah. We'll bring you the best of the best. We've got some operators here right now who will blow your mind."

I moved closer to the door to hear more, but it suddenly yanked open in front of me.

It was Red, and he didn't look happy.

"What the *fuck* are you doing here?"

18

RED

Jesus. Would the woman ever stop getting herself into trouble?

I could put up with a lot. Actually, all us guys could. Part of our training was dealing with the unexpected.

But eavesdropping on a secure video call? With a client? Was she insane?

Not only was she putting one of our biggest missions in danger, she was also putting herself in harm's way.

I gripped her arm much harder than I should have, but I couldn't help it. I didn't care how beautiful she was, how hard my pulse raced every time I saw her, or how hard my dick got at night when I dreamed of her. She just… kept… putting herself in danger.

And that meant putting us in danger, too.

"Ouch, you're hurting me," she cried as I dragged her into my office and slammed the door.

"Take a seat," I commanded her, pointing. Maybe, just maybe, I could talk some sense into her.

She took the chair opposite my desk, rubbing her arm where I'd held her. She'd probably have a bruise later, like she had after the ass spanking we gave her.

"What is your problem?" she asked.

"Are you serious, Mari? What is *my* problem?" I asked, sighing. "Did you know that we have the highest security clearances this country offers? And how hard we had to train and prove ourselves to earn that? Do you know how many times we've put our lives in harm's way for our work? Or how many of us have been injured, and how many we've had to bury, or leave behind in some godforsaken place to be dese-crated by our enemies?"

She shrank into her chair, as if being smaller would make my verbal blows less painful. I knew I'd made my point, and that I needed to shut the hell up, but the anger kept my vitriol flowing.

It had been too long since I'd had anyone who could listen to my pain without just sloughing it off with a war story of their own, or a commiserating shrug. I needed someone to understand the horror of it all. I was uncaged now, and paced my office floor like an angry wild animal. "And you just wander on over here to our *top secret* training facility like you're on a fucking vacation. You shouldn't even *be* here."

She held her head up and sniffled hard. "Well, no one told me I shouldn't come over here, so I didn't see any harm in it. I was thinking of taking a swim up on the roof. I heard your voice and wanted to say hi. I didn't realize what sort of call you were on. Maybe you should soundproof your office or something when you need privacy. Ever think of that?" she asked, leaning forward in her chair and waving her finger.

I loved a woman who could throw her shit around. But this was not the time. Instead, I came around to the front of my desk, and propped a hip on the corner of it.

"Mari, you need to understand the gravity of what goes on around here. You may not have been told explicitly to 'stay out' but c'mon. You're not some dumbass off the street, you're a nurse. Use your better judgment."

"I just want to know what's going on and what I'm getting into. This isn't like a fucking hospital! I don't know the rules."

I stood. "Let's go."

I grabbed her arm again, pulling her up and she stumbled. "Go where? Get off me."

"Look, Mari," I growled lightly, "you can make this easy, or you can make this hard. I suggest you choose easy. We're going back to the cabin."

She tried to pull out of my grip, but I wasn't letting

her go until we were well on our way back. "Fine, I'll go," she protested. "But you don't have to pull me. I can find my way back by myself."

Of course she could. But what was on my mind was what would happen when we got back to the cabin. She had to learn.

The fifteen or so minute walk back went faster than usual because as pissed as Mari was, she was practically race walking. To be honest, I actually had trouble keeping up because of my gimpy leg.

Which was fine with me.

I had the pleasure of watching her ass cheeks jiggle under the camping shorts we guys had gotten her, as well as the muscles of her toned legs as she stepped over the roots and ruts that littered the trail to the house.

"C'mon. Up to your room," I said, holding the front door open for her. "Hustle it up."

"Really? Are you punishing me again?" she asked, annoyed. She put her hands on her hips. "Seriously? Is this what you get off on?"

If she only knew what I got off on. But she'd see in a moment. "Move."

When we got to her room, I sat on the edge of her bed, and beckoned her with a finger. She came over, and stood right in front of me.

"*What?*"

Her defiance was epic. And so was my hard on.

I directed her to stand next to me and in one swift

movement, had her bent over my lap. I held her arms together behind her back, and slipped her shorts down below her ass with my other. She still bore some red marks from her last punishment, which made me nearly cream my jeans.

"Let me up, asshole!" she growled. "Not this shit again!"

I smoothed my large palm over her bum, itching to get started. "I want to hear that you will not invite yourself to the training center again, unless one of us brings you there for a specific reason."

As I rubbed her warm ass, her body responded, and some of her wet excitement made its way to my hand.

"Whatever. Yeah, I promise," she growled through gritted teeth, not quite getting it yet. "Whatever you want, Red. Now get the fuck off me."

Still, that was all I needed. As if on a mechanical spring over which I had no control, my arm flew up and landed a smack on her ass so hard my palm stung.

"Fuuuuck," she shrieked. "Fucking bastard!"

Yes, she was getting a spanking again, but this spanking was going to be a little different than the last one. This one was going to be *Red style*.

"I'll stop… if you say please."

She froze, then pushed back against my hand, groaning and squirming. I ran my hand over the bright red mark I'd just made on her ass, relishing her giving in. The heat from it burned through my hand, and I pressed harder as if to draw it out.

Smack.

The next one came down when she least expected it and when she was in the middle of recovering from the last one.

"Ugggghhhhh," she moaned, her head bucking.

I let that one sit for a moment while I watched her tender flesh turn even brighter red before I soothed her.

And she never did utter *please.*

I repeated the smacks three more times, and by the time I was done, my beautiful Mari was limp as a dishrag, her body trembling from the adrenaline rush. I couldn't hold back any longer, and scooped her up in my arms and wiped a couple tears from her face. She nestled against my neck and caught her breath. "Red—"

But I wasn't done. "One last punishment, Mari. Then… nothing but pleasure."

I picked her up and brought her to her bedroom closet. After clearing space, I carefully set her on the floor and pulled the door closed, locking it.

"Dude, what the fuck is going on up there?" Christian demanded as soon as I returned downstairs.

I settled into one of our club chairs and joined the other guys who must have been done for the day. Crossing my legs to relieve the tension in my groin, I waited until everyone was paying attention to reply.

"She got herself into trouble again. I was on a call about our next mission, and caught her listening in."

"Oh shit," Dutch said. "That girl's got a nose a mile long."

Victor added, "That's not good. What's up with her?"

Exactly.

"She's an amazing woman, I think we would all agree," I declared, seeing nods all around the room. "But she does not exercise the best judgment. And you know how I like to set people straight."

Christian rolled his eyes. "Yeah dude, we also know how you go overboard."

"True dat," Dutch said. "Um, Red, what is that pounding coming from up there right now?"

"I locked her in a closet after spanking her."

Christian jumped to his feet. "You're *fucking* kidding, Red. She's all out of it from a spanking, and you threw her in a small, dark room? That's crossing the line, man!"

Victor leaned forward in his chair and frowned. "Christian's right Dude, we're not on a mission, we can't just tie people up and coerce them the same way we can in-country. Besides, Mari's our… whatever we call her. She's not the enemy."

"I felt I had to take action against the behavior," I explained. "The potential for this next job is off the charts, and she does not need to know anything about it. Or any of our missions, for that matter."

Christian paced the floor. "You're wrong, Red, and you need to calm down with that twitchy hand of yours. She probably had no idea what you were talking about on that call. It was completely out of context for her. You can't do that to her. You learned how to be a better fucking leader than that."

I rubbed my neck.

He headed for the stairs. "I'm going to let her out. This is completely insane."

I jumped up. "Wait, Christian. Let me do it."

He stopped, and looked back at me. I could feel the anger in his eyes, and as I looked around, I realized I'd hurt all the guys. They were right, I'd been taught to be a better leader than this.

"All right. Go, then," Christian said, motioning toward the stairs. This wasn't going to be about Mari as much as it would be about me.

When I reached her room, I knocked on the closet door before I opened it.

"Mari, it's me."

She sniffled, cringing away from me, and it fucking broke my heart. When I offered her my hand, she took it, but I felt unworthy of her touch. Still, this wasn't the room to apologize in, so I brought her to mine as both a change of pace and peace offering.

I tucked her under my thick comforter, and sat on the edge of the bed, facing her.

"Mari, I'm sorry. I went too far."

I really did. God I was a dick.

Wasn't my life already full of enough regrets that I didn't need to add new ones?

She nodded weakly, her lip trembling.

My heart broke again when she reached her hand for mine, her small fingers, dwarfed in my palm. "Why, Red?"

I knew what she was asking, and I swallowed the lump in my throat, looking down. "I... I'm... I don't know. Maybe you can understand if I tell you the story of how I ended up with this limp."

Her eyes widened, and she gave me her attention.

"Okay," she croaked, still a little stronger.

I settled down, and looked at my hands, which were trembling at the memories.

"We were coming back from a training mission on just another sweltering day in the Middle East. We were finishing up at the firebase when gunshots ripped the place up. Turned out we were being ambushed by our host country. They'd decided that they didn't like having us there after all. Several guys were killed, and I took three rounds in my hamstring and hip."

"I'm sorry to hear that," Mari said.

"Well, I'm the lucky one. I might have a limp, I might never run a marathon, but I'm alive. That's a lot more than I can say for my team... some of them had been with us for a while. We'd been friends."

"I'm sorry. Thank you," she said quietly. "For telling me."

"After all this time it still hurts to tell my story," I

admit. "I mean, in our line of work, shit happens all the time. But that one was just so damn unnecessary. Not worth several men's lives. That's when I knew I had to check out for a bit, and the guys invited me to come up here."

"But you were talking about a mission today. I mean, I guess—"

I nod. "More consulting and table top planning than anything else. My days of kicking doors are done. I... I don't like even talking about it."

Mari pushed herself up in my bed. "Well, you sure talked a lot today."

She ran a finger down the bright ink on my forearm, her touch incredibly soothing.

"You're the bright spot, Mari. And what I did... I'm sorry. I was wrong to do what I did... I'm sorry."

She looked into my eyes, then scooted back and lifted the comforter to my bed. "Will you get under the covers with me for a bit?"

Relieved at being given another, undeserved chance, I crawled into the bed, wrapping my arms around her.

Thank god she was willing to hear me out. Not every woman would have.

"I am concerned for your well-being, Mari," I said, quietly when she was snuggled against me. "I'm not a good man, maybe. But the more you're around, the more I like having you around here. If something happened to you, I don't know what I'd do."

"You have a funny way of showing it," she said, slapping my arm.

I deserved that. "I'll promise you that I'll do my best to be a man deserving of your sticking around."

She smiled, and snuggled more against me. "I'll hold you to that, mister. Deal."

19

MARI

NO ONE HAD EVER TOLD ME EXACTLY WHAT THEY wanted cleaned, or how often they wanted it done, so I thought I'd better figure it out for myself before things got stupid. I didn't want any more trouble.

Actually, after Red apologized, there had been no more punishments. Oh, I still got a swat on the butt from time to time, but it was all for fun, not punishment. I never quite knew when my ass was going to be a target for one of the four guys I lived with. Made life interesting.

But I guess I was equally as naughty—good naughty, of course—judging from the way those spankings turned me on.

It was the strangest thing. I'd never gone that far before, yet with these four I never seemed to have any line I wasn't willing to cross. And the guys seemed to be getting off on them, as well, from the looks of the big erections they sported.

I moved through the library with a vacuum I'd found in a closet, and a dust rag tucked into the pocket of an apron I'd found in the pantry. I suppose I looked like a proper cleaning lady, even if I was doing what was probably a crappy job. Still, based off the crackling sound of dirt, dust, and other stuff I picked up, I was helping in a small way.

I really did miss my job and friends. But I didn't know whether it was safe to go back home yet. I mean, I guess I *could* go home at any time, but wouldn't that make me just a sitting duck, waiting for the gang-bangers to eventually find me? Because they would.

And my nursing job, which I wanted to go back to, as well. I really did love the patients—well, most of them. There was nothing like advocating for them, solving mysterious health puzzles, or the adrenaline rush of helping someone sick feel better. And I was always learning something new. *That* I was really starting to miss. I mean, sitting around Savage Mountain with four hunky men had its benefits—big benefits, if you got my gist— but if I didn't find something to do with my brain soon, I was afraid it would rot.

As much as I'd enjoyed the cabin—overlooking the unpleasantries of being accused of stealing—I needed to make a plan to get back to civilization and deal with my problems, put them to bed, and move on.

And my first step was to get in touch with Luci.

That night when I came down for dinner, I stood at the head of the table and waited until I had everyone's attention.

"Mari, is there something on your mind?" Christian asked.

I nodded and smiled. "There is, Christian, thank you for asking."

I looked around, making sure I had the rapt attention of each of them. Each of the fucking gorgeous, walking hunks of male perfection.

I'd really miss them when I was gone.

"I need to get in touch with my friend Luci at home. It's been too long, and I'm sure she's worried sick about me."

I took a deep breath mustering all the guts I could.

"I'd like to contact her tomorrow, from your office, Red, since I know you have Skype there. What's a good time for you?"

Talk about asking for the sale. I was on *fire…*

They looked at each other, and then back to me.

"That's fine, Mari. How about nine a.m.?" Red asked. "Um, it's not Skype though. We use a more secure system."

What? Was that a yes? No resistance? I must have heard wrong.

"No Skype?"

"No, but I can install it if that's your preference."

I took a deep breath to make sure he wasn't teasing me. "Guys, this is really important to me. I'm sure you understand."

They looked at each other again, then back at me, nodding slightly.

I leaned forward on the dining table, pushing my boobs together a bit. I was prepared to do what I had to.

"So what do you say?"

Christian raised his eyebrows, smirking. "Mari, I think Red gave you an answer."

Oh. Guess the girls were unneeded.

"Well. Great. Let's have dinner then."

***

I GOT up at the crack of dawn so I could catch Luci before she went to work, and bugged Red until he gave up with a laugh and walked me to his office an hour early just to make sure Skype worked.

After coffee, I sat at Red's desk, impressed by the understated comfort of his office chair while he watched me from the other side of the room, smiling at my excitement over connecting with my friend.

Promptly at seven, I clicked call, and Skype made that funny ringing sound it did. Luci answered.

"Hello?" she said, her voice full of sleep.

"Luce, it's me!" I cried.

There was silence for a moment. I looked at Red, who nodded. I loved that guy.

Oh shit. Did I just say *love*?

"Wha? Mari? Is that you?" Luci shrieked. "Where the fuck are you?"

"It's me, it's me. How are ya girlfriend?" I tried to hide my crackling voice. I hadn't realized what an effect her familiar voice would have on me.

"Oh my god, Mari. What the fuck? Where are you? Are you okay?"

"I'm with some guys who picked me up at a truck stop and fought off one of the gangbangers the night I left." I didn't want to be too specific, and to make sure I'd kept things vague enough, I looked up at Red, who nodded his approval.

"Whoa… so you're okay?"

"I'm fine, Luci, perfectly safe and sound. How are you?"

"Oh Mari. Well, you know how shit goes, things have been kind of crazy. My cousin insisted for the longest time that I tell him where you were, but he finally believed I didn't know."

I rolled my eyes, making Red laugh silently.

She continued. "Then, the guy who headed up the gang, the one who wanted you… you know… well, he's *dead*. That's right. One morning he just ended up dead."

Jesus. I might have fallen down had I not been sitting in Red's chair.

Holy fuck.

I was afraid to ask the question streaming through my mind, whether he was dead due to the work of the guys here on the mountain? Had they pulled some long and dangerous strings that could get rid of people who were bad news?

Actually, I think I knew the answer to that.

"Um, wow, Luci. That's crazy." I kept staring at my hands, terrified to look anywhere else.

"Mari, you can come home now. And if you don't come back soon, you'll lose your job at the hospital," Luci said, jolting me out of my head. "With that guy gone, I think you're safe. Come back. You *need* to come back. I tried to talk the hospital into putting you on a leave of absence, but they need someone to cover your shifts."

Okay, that did it. I loved my job. I couldn't lose it like that, like some sort of slacker who abandoned her responsibilities. Since the asshole who'd been after me was gone, I could go home.

I was essentially free.

"Okay, Luce. Tell them I'll be home soon. In fact, I'll get back to you and let you know when to expect me. And Luci, thank you for taking all that up for me."

I finally looked up to find Red doodling on the pad before him. His brows were knit and his lips were pressed together tightly. It was safe to say, he didn't look happy at my mention of going home.

Now it was time for Luci's voice to break. "No, Mari. You saved me. I'm the one who owes you thanks."

My heart swelled. I was proud of defending my friend. Fuck that guy who'd attacked her. He deserved to be dead.

"Okay, sweetie, I gotta go. But I'll get back in touch soon," I told her.

My heart broke a little bit at the thought of saying goodbye to her.

But I closed the call. I had shit to do.

The rest of that day passed like all the others before it, with my finding a couple things to clean to stay busy. But this time I'd been formulating a plan.

"Hey, can I get you guys some coffee?" I cheerfully asked the next morning, ignoring that Leeann was already in the kitchen and that she usually took care of that task.

Before she could reach it, I grabbed the coffee pot off the warmer, brought it over to the dining table, and began pouring. She slammed something in the kitchen behind me. I was so used to her passive aggressive tantrums, I didn't even turn around.

"Mari, do you have anything to tell us yet about the silver box?" Victor asked, his voice level.

If he wasn't so goddamn gorgeous in his neatly trimmed beard and watch cap, I might have smacked the smug off his face.

I spilled a puddle of coffee on the table.

Deep breath. Take a deep breath, I told myself.

But it didn't help.

"Are you guys still on that bullshit?" I snapped.

Whoops.

But I might as well really dig my grave deep.

So I doubled down. "Do you really think I'd want that box? Seriously. I can buy my own fucking boxes. In fact—"

I looked around. Their mouths were pretty much hanging open.

"—how about I *pay* you guys for that box? Just to call it even. I'll buy it from you to put all this bullshit to an end."

I marched over to the living room table where the box in question was displayed, and brought it back to the dining table, where I plunked it down.

"How much you want for it? Ten bucks? A hundred bucks? Hell, I'll give you a thousand bucks for the piece of shit if you'd get off my back about it."

They were still silent, and my fury was raging. There was no stopping me now.

"For weeks now, I've shouldered all your bullshit. Your PTSD, your paranoia, your twisted sense of how to treat a woman. And you know what? I won't lie, part of it I've enjoyed. All four of you fuck like champs, and I don't think I've ever had such a sexual workout. But the whole fucking time, you pin this box shit on me. Well fuck that, because I didn't do it. So I'm just gonna end this shit. And you know what I'm gonna do with the box when I finally own it? I'm gonna take the huge sledgehammer out in the tool shed, and DEMOLISH IT."

Okay, now I was shouting. Take it down a notch, girl.

"Um, Mari, you really don't have to throw a tantrum like that—" Dutch started to say.

"Shut the fuck up, Dutch." I picked up the box again, squeezing it so hard I nearly dented it. "Another thing, guys. If this is soooo valuable, why is it sitting out in the open? Why isn't it kept someplace safe?"

Christian spoke up. "It *is* someplace safe. In our house. We just don't expect thieves to be walking through."

There was just no getting through to them.

I grabbed my own cup of coffee and left to have breakfast in my bedroom. It was time to give myself a grown-up time out. I paused at the door though, and looked back at them. "Fuck you guys. All of you."

I CAME DOWN that evening after I'd heard the guys retire to their rooms. I'd even peered down the stairs to make sure creepy Leeann had vacated. I was getting stir crazy hanging out in my room except to get food and go right back up.

I plopped on the soft living room sofa and opened the *Elle* magazine the guys had brought me from their last trip to civilization. I was flattered they'd thought I was so stylish, but to be honest I hadn't read a fashion magazine since I'd been in college. My daily fashion choices consisted of choosing between green scrubs and blue scrubs. Oh, and whether I'd wear sneakers or Dansko clogs. That was it.

But *Elle* had some fun horoscopes, and that's what I was going for when I heard the front door quietly open and close. I crunched myself flat on the sofa, still in a shitty mood, wondering who the hell hadn't gone to bed yet.

The sofa I'd chosen faced a huge bay window with a view of the yard and forest beyond, which meant it was turned away from the rest of the room. It was a perfect place to hide. I wouldn't have to interact with anyone.

Also, perfect place from which to spy.

Peeking over the cushion, who should I spy tiptoeing around, but Leeann.

Why was she at the house so late? Did she have something to prep for breakfast?

I peered over the sofa arm and watched her quietly move through the room and head to the bottom of the stairs. There, she stopped, cocking her ear as if to ascertain who might still be up.

Satisfied with the silence, she moved through the house with a stealthy intention.

And wouldn't you know, she stuffed that pain in the ass Persian box right under her shirt, and scurried back to the front door.

Really? Was she going to plant that goddamn thing on me *again*?

Not this time, Miss Pissy Pots and Pans.

"STOP. WHERE THE FUCK ARE YOU GOING?" I yelled at the top of my voice, sitting up and startling the shit out of her.

She froze, and turned to me with disbelieving eyes.

I was about to become her worst nightmare.

"Fuck you, slut," she finally growled.

Really? Was that the best she could do?

"WHERE ARE YOU GOING WITH THAT BOX? ARE YOU GONNA PLANT IT ON ME AGAIN?" I called out, making as much noise as I could. I kept the couch between us, though. Who knew how much of Dutch's martial arts classes she'd completed.

And just as I'd hoped, lights were flicking on, and bedroom doors were opening. Heavy footsteps thundered down the stairs toward us, and I grinned in triumph as Leeann realized she'd been caught.

"What the hell is going on?" Victor asked. "We're trying to get some sleep."

I pointed to Leeann, who stood there about as guilty as a person could get.

"Ask her. She's stealing the box, probably to plant on me. *Again.*"

Part of me wanted to rip that nasty bitch's hair out. But I promised myself that I would be the adult in all this… at least, I swore I did until I took a step towards her, and Dutch laid a powerful hand on my shoulder.

"Leeann, what are you doing?" he asked.

"Um. Nothing," she said in a small voice, obviously guilty as hell.

Red walked over and took the box from her. "Did you steal this last time, and plant it in Mari's things?"

She looked down at her empty hands, then from one guy to the next. For a moment I felt sorry for her. She seemed so alone, having to resort to something so juvenile to turn them against me.

She nodded.

Dutch walked over to the front door and opened it. "Okay Leeann. Go back to your room and pack up. We'll be driving you to town tomorrow.

She nodded quickly and ran out the door. Dutch closed it behind her and locked it.

All eyes were on me.

The moment I'd been waiting for. *Yes.*

"Seems we owe you an apology, Mari. A big one," Victor said, turning the box over in his hands. It was as if he were wondering how a little thing could cause so much trouble.

Like the dead houseplant I'd used to save Luci.

20

CHRISTIAN

"You really don't have to clean my room," I told Mari, even though I certainly enjoyed the sight of her doing so.

She was puttering around my bedroom, wearing wonderfully snug yoga pants and some sort of sports top that showcased her figure brilliantly.

Honestly, I hoped she'd keep cleaning, just so I could keep watching her. In my line of work, I encountered plenty of women who were in shape. I encountered plenty who were confident badasses. But none of them had ever had the effect on me that Mari did. Something about her effortless confidence and fuck-you attitude, combined with a certain amount of vulnerability, made my motor rev.

And of course, her body was what the gods intended when they created women. Her long wavy hair was pulled into a messy confection at the back of her neck, where loose curls cascaded down her back. She occasionally stopped to push a couple sweaty strands off her forehead, and look over at me with her green eyes.

She shrugged. "I don't have anything else to do. Might as well be useful," she said, pulling a book off my shelf and staring at the spine.

"Was this good?" she asked, holding out one of my books on U.S. history. *Wilderness At Dawn: The Settling of the North American Continent.*

I plopped down on the bed. If she was going to continue, I was going to be comfortable.

"Yeah. If you like history. Which I do," I said.

She nodded, and I could see her lips twitch in an interested murmur as she read the inner flyleaf, nodding to herself.

God, a girl who liked history. Shoot me now, because it didn't get any better than that.

She flipped through the first few pages. "May I borrow it?"

"Maybe."

She put her hands on her hips, her face clouded with irritation. "You need some collateral as proof I'll bring it back? How 'bout that silver box in your living room?"

"Oh Christ, *that* thing," I said, waving it off and trying to show her I was just teasing a second ago. "I hope I never have to see it again."

Seriously. What a fiasco.

"Oh, I don't know about that. I'm going to make sure that is a centerpiece of your living room décor so I can make you feel guilty and miserable for the rest of your life."

Her words were pointed, but as her face broke out in a smile, I could tell she was bullshitting. "Yeah well, so far you're doing a great job."

She sashayed over, sitting on the edge of my bed.

"Good. From now on, that will be my top goal in life. To make you feel like shit."

"Well then, I guess I have nothing to look forward to," I ran a finger down her arm, pulling the dust rag out of her hand and tossing it to the floor. "I'll just have to find some tolerable existence in other distractions."

Mari shivered, and leaned into my touch. "Christian, how come you're not at the training center?"

I pointed to my watch. "It's Saturday. You losing track of time?"

She nodded, pulling away slightly. "I guess I am. It's probably time for me to head back to civilization, now that the threat seems gone."

Her words hit me hard. I thought back to the first time Dutch and I'd seen her at the truck stop diner. There'd been no doubt she was terrified and in complete survival mode, but there'd been something in her eyes that said she'd fight to the death.

I rolled to my side, and pulled her to me.

"Mari, we don't want you to leave."

She flipped to her back and looked up at the ceiling.

"I wouldn't want me to leave, either." She laughed out loud, slapping the bed at her joke.

I gently pulled her face toward mine. "I'm serious."

She looked into my eyes, and swallowed. "Christian, I get it. I wouldn't want my cleaning lady to leave, either. But this was never a long-term gig for me. You know that better than anyone. I'm not sure I… fit here."

Christ, sometimes she was thickheaded. Who cared about the cleaning?

"Mari, I'm not talking about wanting you to stick around just to clean the house. I want you to stay because… I've grown attached to you. We all have."

She exhaled slowly, her humor dropping away as I saw inside her heart. "Well, I have something to admit. I've grown attached to you guys, too. In spite of all that has happened." She nudged me hard in the ribs.

Which I deserved.

"Don't joke about that, Mari. Please. It's the biggest fuckup I've made in a long time."

"Okay. But if I were to stay, I'd feel compelled to choose one of you," she says, cupping my cheek. "And I could never do that. Each of you is special. Each of you… is a tremendous man. And while I know you guys have been fine when we've all just been casual, I couldn't choose one and hurt the remaining three. Nope, no way."

I sighed. Couldn't really argue with that.

But I could take off her clothes and ravish her, enjoying the time we had left.

I pushed myself up, straddling her waist and holding her arms above her head. She pulled and twisted, grinning and laughing.

"I think you like being restrained."

"Maybe… " she said, biting her lip. "You guys have shown me a few sides to myself I didn't know existed."

"Goes both ways," I said as I moved off her long enough to pull her top over her head and strip her pants down. I immediately buried my face in her bare pussy, licking deeply as I reached up to massage her tits.

"Christian…" she moaned, running her fingers through my hair. She tasted so goddamn good it was all I could do to resist blowing my wad. Her tangy sweetness and the sounds she was making would drive any man over the edge.

But I had to hold off. I had plans for my dick.

"Uhhhh," she moaned when I fluttered the tip of my tongue over her erect clit. "God, Christian, where did you learn to do that?"

She shimmied her hips harder into my face as I licked her from clit to asshole and back, all while pushing her lush tits together and rubbing my thumbs over her hard nipples.

Her entire body began to shudder, her thighs clamping and releasing, and I knew she was close. I zeroed in on her clit and sucked hard, the intense sensation sending her over the edge. Her head rocked back and forth, her fists pounding the bed.

"Oh god, Christian, I'm coming. Yeah… I'm coming now!" she cried, her breaths coming in long, uneven rasps.

I pulled my face out of her soaked pussy and dropped my jeans and T-shirt on the floor. Stretching a condom I'd grabbed from my pocket over my cock, I pressed myself against her hungry opening. I hesitated, knowing she'd come again, fast and hard. I needed to make myself last for her.

Mari saw, and spread her legs wider, wrapping her ankles around me. "It's okay… I'm ready."

I pushed just my head inside, and couldn't help but moan from the exquisite pulse of her inner walls, getting ready for the pounding I was about to give her. I pushed her arms up, pinning them against the bed, and started to thrust.

My first plunge was hard, direct, and deep. I wanted her to remember this day and how I'd made her feel. I knew I'd never forget how she made me feel.

Fuck, I'd only known her a short time, and if she left now…

Not the time to be thinking about shit like that.

I leaned forward and sealed my mouth to hers. Her tongue flicked against mine as I taunted her with the delicious taste of her own pussy. Our lips would be sore later, as hungry as we both were. Shit, everything was going to be sore later.

"I fucking love being inside you, beautiful girl," I whispered, pulling back to watch her face. I kept hammering, and her eyes swam as tremors flooded her body. She was overwhelmed, and I couldn't hold back either. My voice had grown guttural as my balls tightened and all sensation centered around my groin. A giant eruption was building, and I was ready for it.

I let go of her wrists, bracing myself on the mattress, and she put her hands on either side of my face, giving me the slightest smile just as I exploded. I roared like a wild man, fucking her so fast and hard it was a miracle we didn't go flying off the bed.

"Oh god," she murmured. "God, I want more… "

That's my girl.

"Hey, you horndogs forgot to close the bedroom door," Dutch said, standing there, looking at Mari's flushed complexion. "You trying to put on a show?"

She laughed weakly. "Well, maybe we didn't want anyone to feel left out. Besides, I bet you loved staring at Chris' flexing ass, didn't you?"

"C'mon in, Dutch. This will be like the night I met you two," she said.

Dutch didn't have to be asked twice. He entered the room and started unbuckling his belt.

"Well, um, the night we met, I don't remember

anything like *this*," he said, palming himself thickly, his cock already hard and ready for her.

I rolled away, staying next to Mari as Dutch stepped closer, his eyes fixed on the beautiful sight in front of him.

"Sit on the edge of the bed," he told her. She obeyed, putting her hands on either side of his hips, inhaling his cock deeply as soon as she could.

I watched, my eyes fixed on Mari as Dutch went balls-deep in a matter of seconds. He wove his fingers into her hair, but she was in total control of him, her fingers digging into his ass as she pulled herself tighter and tighter, bobbing up and down to massage and pleasure him with everything she had. She squeezed her eyes shut as they teared, and pistoned back and forth until his growls rose to a crescendo. He pulled out just in time to spurt all over her face and chest, his seed gleaming like pearls on her skin.

"Fuck *me*," he hollered, stroking himself dry on her flushed skin.

She smiled up at him with his cum all over her, one of the hottest fucking things I'd ever seen. She was so happy with the pleasure she'd granted.

'Course he was happy, too.

"Hey, y'all need to keep down the sex noise up here." Victor stood in the doorway laughing, with Red behind him, peering over his shoulder.

They didn't wait for an invitation. They didn't need to. The single look on Mari's cum stained face and the way she licked her lips told them everything they needed to know.

"On your knees," Red told her as he pulled on a condom.

Victor positioned himself right in front of her, and the two tag-teamed my girl.

Our girl.

I watched as she came again around Red's cock, moaning thickly with a mouthful of Victor's cream. I was hoping she'd realize she had a life with us, even as my cock stood up for more attention, and decide to stay on Savage Mountain with us.

21

MARI

I opened the French doors to my bedroom balcony to see the last of the sun going down, the sky a dramatic burning red on the horizon. The din of crickets and other creatures just getting warmed up for the night was rising by the minute as we humans were closing ourselves in. I just had to have one more whiff of the piney mountain air before sealing myself in for the night.

When I did, and turned back to my luxurious bedroom, my gaze settled on the massive bunch of wildflowers one of the guys had pulled together for me. Dutch had stuffed them into a huge mason jar, perfectly in keeping with the rustic chic of the cabin. I swore I'd never received a better gift.

Made by hand.

Made with love.

I vibrated, thinking back to when I'd slept with not two of the guys, nor just three, but ALL four of them in Christian's room.

It was a story I'd probably carry to my grave. I mean, that was some kinky shit, messing around with all of them.

Four loads... four men, whose slight, natural dishevelment sent my pulse racing every time I saw them.

Every. Single. Time.

And as smoking hot as they were in their mountain man gear, they were ten times more so when they were undressed.

Christian—my salt and pepper, blue-eyed love, haunted so badly by whatever sheer hell he'd seen, that he lived in fear of hurting someone in the middle of the night without realizing it. I'd never gotten the full story of why he had someone lock him in his room at night. Maybe I never would.

Then there was Dutch, the Herculean knight in shining armor-slash-medical doctor who'd taken down my pursuer with one swing of his arm that night in the truck stop diner. He'd seen the terror in my eyes and refused to leave me behind. And to find out he'd built his own fantasy treehouse. What was there not to love?

Victor, my untamed James Bond in a flannel shirt and watch cap, a study in contrasts with his perfectly trimmed beard, and hideous scars crisscrossing his back. His sniper skills had served many purposes and earned him a lot of money, but the emotional price he'd paid was high. He'd seen the worst of human nature, but somehow managed to remember mostly the good.

Last—my ginger hunk, Red. Bright sleeve tattoos wove around his muscular arms, expressing his inner self more than the few words he spoke ever would. He kept his issues as quiet as he was. Even his limp was barely perceptible. And yet he did anything but fade into the woodwork, his presence something to be reckoned with, just like his smoldering sensuality.

They wanted me to stay. All four of them.

But it just wasn't possible.

Choosing among them was not something I was willing to do. Nor was it something I was *able* to do.

I had tears in my eyes just thinking about it, when my weighty thoughts were interrupted by some sort of commotion on the floor below. Heavy footsteps ran back and forth and urgent voices filtered up the stairs.

"Hey guys, what's up?" I asked, descending the steps in a hurried trot.

When I got to the kitchen, it was pretty clear what was going on. I sprang into nurse mode when I saw the deep gash on Dutch's arm, oozing blood all over the floor.

"Do you have a medical kit here in the house?" I

asked, grabbing a clean dishtowel and pressing it on his forearm. It wasn't much, but it was a start.

"Y… yeah. In my room," he said, his face already going pale.

"Vic, will you go get Dutch's doctor bag? And Christian, will you bring a chair over?"

"Yup," Christian said, but when he brought it over I shook my head, having changed my mind.

"Let's get Dutch onto the table, I don't want him in shock." The dishtowel was already soaked, so I grabbed another.

The guys responded as if they'd been training for something like this, which I supposed they had. No worries about mess, no posturing, just efficient action.

"Okay, that'll work," I said, when he was up on the table. "When the bleeding is staunched, I can give him stitches. Tell me what happened."

Dutch shook his head. "I was chopping wood, getting some kindling ready for tonight. The piece I was cutting caught the blade and drove it right into my arm."

Victor put the doctor bag down next to me.

Red returned with more towels. "Want me to apply pressure while you look for what you need?"

I let him take over, and when I started fishing through Dutch's bag, I realized my hands were shaking. I'd sewn up wounds many times, but never on someone I cared for.

Yes, I cared for him. I cared for all of them.

"I didn't know nurses could do stitches," Christian said.

"Advance practice nurses can," I replied, letting my mind shut down a little to push away the fear. "Sometime I'll tell you all the levels. Dutch, I found the suturing materials in your bag. But your anesthetic is out of date."

He looked over, then lay his head back. "Shit. When I recently resupplied, I only worried about the school's supplies, not my personal bag. Guess you're gonna have to stitch me without any numbing."

I looked at him with a raised eyebrow. He might be a big, tough military man, but I'd seen men like him faint from less.

"Told you assholes it would be great to have a nurse around!" he said, laying his head back and closing his eyes. "You'd have just killed me by now."

"Well, you're a fucking doctor, and what good is that doing us?" Victor asked, amused.

"Dude, I can't stitch myself—"

I held my hands up after snapping on the surgical gloves I'd found in the bag. "Okay. I need all of you to quiet down right now," I said, taking charge. "Red, keep pressure on the arm. And Victor, go get some booze from the cabinet. Strong stuff, and pour Dutch a shot."

"Dutch courage," Victor joked as he poured a tumbler and held Dutch's head up to help him toss it back. After downing the big shot of whiskey, Dutch laid his head back and let me get to work.

I felt terrible about the great pain he was in, but he took it well, swallowing his grunts and groans. Funny, because doctors were usually the biggest sissies.

"How will you teach your martial arts class with stitches in your arm?" I asked to distract him.

He winced as I put in the last couple stitches. "I… I'll be able to pull something off. Or maybe you might get off your dead ass for once, Christian?"

Christian chuckled. "Maybe."

When I was finished, I bandaged Dutch's arm, put a small pillow from the sofa under his head, and washed up.

"Hey, while I have all of you here, I wanted to say something."

Christian put his hands on his hips. "What is it, Mari?"

Dutch reached over and took my hand with his good one. It was so warm, I wanted to cry.

"I want you to know how much I appreciate all you've done for me, especially asking me to stay."

I swallowed hard. I was *not* going to get choked up. If I was going to start bawling, it would have to wait until I was back in my room.

Victor raised his eyebrows. "Sounds ominous. What's up, baby?"

"I'd like to stay. I really would. I've gotten attached to each of you. Actually, more than attached. And that's the problem."

I looked around the dining table at all their handsome faces.

Was I about to make the mistake of my life?

"But I've decided not to stay, because I will not choose. I told Christian the other day, I can't pick one guy and hurt the other three. I'd rather be alone than live with having done something like that."

Red cleared his throat. "Well, Mari, you don't have to really look at it that way—"

"I do, Red," I interrupted. "I really do. I'd rather have one broken heart and four friends remain together than wrecking what you all have. And if you'll excuse me, I need to return to my room. Dutch, holler if you need anything for that arm."

Without waiting for any of them to respond, I hustled toward the stairs.

They didn't need to see the tears streaming down my face.

22

DUTCH

D AMN IF OUR HOT LITTLE NURSE DIDN'T COME THROUGH in a pinch.

I looked down at the bandage on my arm, impressed. I might have been able to suture my own arm, but it would have been tough. And to be honest, judging from the stitches Mari had carefully placed, she'd done a far better job than I could have.

After she'd run off to her room, we guys took the opportunity to talk about our current situation. Victor and Red helped me off the dining table and to the sofa. I was a little woozy with shock and booze, but moving helped.

Christian started pacing, like he often did, while Red and Victor took seats in their favorite easy chairs.

"We can't lose her. I mean, why can't she stay without choosing one of us?" Christian said, starting things off. "I'm happy to share her with all of you. We're going to be in and out for work, and most of the time not together. I'll be glad for a backup."

I had to laugh at that one.

"I'm good with that," Victor said.

Red and Christian nodded.

I was okay with it, too.

"Where did she get the idea she had to pick, anyway?" I asked, not expecting an answer from anyone.

But it turned out I was getting an answer from Mari, who'd come back down the stairs without us hearing her.

"Hey," she said, taking a seat on one of the living room's club chairs. Mine, in fact, since I was sprawled on the sofa with my arm elevated.

"Baby, we were just saying you didn't have to choose among us," Victor said.

She frowned, confused. "Huh? What does that mean?"

Red spoke up. "Stay with us. Stay with us all. You don't have to choose one of us. We… we need you. Not me, not Chris, not Dutch, not Vic. We. All of us."

Her mouth dropped open as she looked from one of us to the other, our proposal turning over in her mind.

I leaned sat up on the couch, cradling my aching arm. "Think about it. You don't have to decide right now, or even tomorrow. But if you do stay, we can add first aid to our training curriculum, and put you in charge of that."

A slow smile crossed her face. "Can I go on a job? With one of you guys?"

Always making a deal, this one.

"Well, you'd have to go through the full training. Do you have anything in your background you are hiding?"

She took a deep breath. "You mean like killing someone? Yeah, with a houseplant apparently. Small detail, but I'm sure that won't hold me back!"

"Well, Mari," I continued, "think about our offer. I can speak for all the guys when I say we'd love to have you join our little family."

She stood up and my heart sank. I braced myself for bad news.

"I don't have to think about it," she said.

I glanced at Christian, who'd pressed his lips together.

"I accept."

We all looked at each other.

"Um, what?" Victor asked.

"I accept. I'll stay with you." She looked around, taking each one of us in. "I'll stay with all of you. I love you."

Her words brought smiles to our faces, and Christian swept her up, spinning her around twice before carrying her over to each of us in turn for a kiss.

And she kissed us all right back. In spite of my now-throbbing arm, it had turned out to be a fucking great day.

23

VICTOR

She wasn't the best student. Mari had a scrappy attitude that helped in self-defense, but her shooting took time to come up to par. Still, being around us all the time meant she absorbed physical fitness almost through osmosis and her class work was superb.

The only thing she wasn't that great at was figuring out when to be quiet and listen. On a job, there were a lot of times that people wouldn't take her questions well.

But her combination of brains and beauty just slayed me, so I couldn't really complain.

Her contribution to the training center was a kick-ass upgrade to our first aid course, something we desperately needed. Dutch admitted his doctor's point of view went over a lot of heads, and Mari's straightforward style, ditching the jargon for the basics, connected better with people who needed the down and dirty for when medics or docs were not available.

I was lucky enough to take her with me on her first job, undercover work where we traveled as husband and wife.

Of course we shared a room. Because, work, you know.

We were in Panama, where a wealthy man from Ohio had made off with the toddler he'd had with his ex-wife. Turned out he wasn't happy with the visitation rights granted him by the courts, so he took the matter into his own hands, kidnapping the girl and taking her out of the country.

Not a good move.

Mari and I posed as American tourists visiting the country with a university group. We ditched the tour as soon as we found him, disabled his security detail, and grabbed the kid. In and out in just under a week. Dad came home to the States in handcuffs, and Mari delivered the little one right into her mother's arms.

Lots of tears were shed, and I'm not too proud to admit that not all of them were female.

Of course I knew Mari was a nurse and all, but what got me was how great she was with the kid. She did such a good job of calming her throughout the whole ordeal, the child emerged as trauma-free as one could hope.

I was so proud of my girl. She followed protocol and used her skills like a champ.

To celebrate our success, we rented an insanely cool house on a cliff in Costa Rica for a few days before returning home. It had a heated infinity pool that overlooked the ocean, airy cotton decor, and natural lighting that seemed to highlight Mari at every turn.

I couldn't have asked for a better way to wind down after a mission that was admittedly made a bit more stressful by it being Mari's first time out of the gate.

The minute we got there, I threw my suitcase on the bed, popped open a beer, and opened the sliding glass doors facing the ocean. A warm, salty breeze filled the house in moments, and the tension I'd been carrying began to melt away. I whipped my shirt off, pulled on my sunglasses, and plopped into a lounge chair.

"Mari!" I hollered.

I'd left her to explore the house. I was more interested in taking a load off and checking out the blue water.

"Here I am," she called.

I turned to see what had been taking her so long. Turned out, not much.

She stood in a bright pink string bikini bottom that fit her like a second skin.

And that was *all* she wore. The whole thing couldn't have weighed four ounces total

Her luxurious hair fell in waves over her shoulders, lifted occasionally by the sea breeze. As she walked toward me in her bare feet, she stepped carefully on the warm pool deck, her breasts swaying with every step.

My erection practically tore through the thin cotton of my tropical weight pants, I stiffened up so fast.

I tore my eyes away for a second to assess our surroundings, first, because I always did things like that, and two, to check our privacy.

There was no one around as far as I could see. We could do whatever the hell we wanted.

And I planned to do just that.

I stood from my lounge chair, and dropped my pants. My hard dick bounced when it was finally free, and I immediately palmed myself to get things under control.

"Damn, baby, turn around," I said.

She took her time rotating, watching me over her shoulder and knowing just what she was doing. Naturally, her backside was just as stunning as her front, and the upside down heart of her ass made my pulse race. I walked up behind her and cupped her juicy bum, squeezing while I pressed my cock into her.

She stretched her arms over her shoulders and reached back, placing a hand on either side of my head while I kissed her soft neck. The ocean air and warm sun was a balm for the danger we'd faced together, and a reward for reuniting a little girl with her mom.

We deserved this. We deserved each other. And the good news was, Mari had so much love to give, there was enough for all us guys.

But at the moment, they were at home on the mountain, and she and I were chilling in Costa Rica. I hoped to fuck her so much that on returning home, I was desperate for a break. The other guys could take over where I'd left off.

Lucky for us, she was as insatiable as we were.

"Lie down, baby," I said, guiding her to a big double lounge chair.

I untied the bows holding the bikini on her curvy hips, and threw the small scrap of fabric aside. In the sunlight, her skin shone, and when I pushed her legs apart, her pussy glistened. I buried my face there, desperate for a taste of her sweet excitement. With my hands on the backs of her thighs, I took the opportunity to lift her legs until her ass was level with my face. I settled my mouth against her most private place, and she responded by grabbing my shoulders as leverage to grind her hips into me, leaving her shuddering on a warm day.

I couldn't wait any longer to be inside this woman. I didn't know how many times we'd fucked on our mission, but today, as every other, was like being with her for the first time.

I pulled her legs up over my shoulders and drove deep inside her, holding myself while I caught my breath. Her gaze was fixed on mine, and didn't waver as I rocked my hips in and out, relishing the way her inner walls milked me. She smelled like clean girl with just a hint of sex. That, with her tits bouncing from my hard thrusts, took my breath away.

"Oh god, more Vic, please," she said between gasps, her voice throaty and raw. "God, I fucking love you."

We rocked until the chair scraped on the deck, and I gasped, my heart hammering in my chest. Mari tightened around me, and I knew she was close. My balls drew in as my cock expanded, and I devoted myself to giving her an unforgettable climax. I lost myself pounding into her with a furious passion, and I unloaded with a holler.

"So fucking great..." I growled, my sweat dripping onto the lounge chair below.

Mari caught her breath. "Looks like I might be wearing you out." She laughed.

Yeah, like that could ever happen.

CHAPTER 24

MARI

My first mission had been scary, exciting, and ultimately very satisfying. I was back on my game, doing something that helped people. The rush I'd gotten from returning a little girl to her mother was akin to saving a life in the hospital.

There was nothing like it.

But it took a lot out of you. I was grateful to have a few days to unwind with Victor in Costa Rica, and even more grateful to be back on the mountain.

With my guys. All four of them.

There were congratulations all around when I returned, and champagne was poured liberally.

"Guys, you should have seen Mari with that little girl. She kept the kid so calm the whole time, she never shed a tear." Victor shook his head like he still couldn't believe how well everything had been handled.

Christian raised his glass to mine. "I'm not surprised. We knew you were a badass the night we picked you up in the truck stop. We just pretended you really wanted to clean our house." He laughed and looked at Dutch as they remembered.

"Well, I recall Dutch whooping that guy's ass, the one who was after me. And the rest... well, what happened to Leeann?"

The downside of Leeann's leaving was that the cooking fell on our shoulders now. But we rotated nights. It really wasn't so bad.

Dutch shook his head, and the others echoed the maneuver. Finally, Chris spoke up. "We gave her a generous severance package to keep her quiet, and that's the end of it. You're the only woman on the mountain now, Queen of Savage Mountain."

I liked the sound of that. "Either way, it felt really good to help that little girl and her mom. Kind of made me want to have my own little person to look after," I said.

My effort to test the waters was about as unsubtle as could be. I smiled brightly as I looked from one guy to the next as their eyebrows rose.

"Cheers to that," Christian said, clinking glasses with everyone. "Mari, you would make an awesome mother."

"Good thing someone thinks so," I mumbled, smelling my bubbly.

Red leaned toward me. "What was that Mari? What did you say?"

Dutch nodded. "You heard her dude."

Yeah. He did.

"Are you trying to tell us something?" Red asked.

I smiled coyly, putting down my champagne after one little sip. Silly men, they never noticed anything.

"Hey Dutch, do you think you could get me some seltzer water?" I asked. "Or ginger ale?"

Christian smacked his forehead with his hand. "Holy fuck."

If I didn't know better, I'd swear there were tears in his eyes.

Red rushed me, picking me up and spinning me around the room as Dutch and Victor high-fived and hugged each other.

"Yeah guys, you're going to be fathers," I shouted, my voice quavering with pride. I'd hoped they'd be happy about my unexpected pregnancy but you just never knew how something like that would go.

"Which one of us is the dad?" Dutch asked. "I mean, I guess we can't tell yet, but—"

"You all are," I said, looking from one stunning man to the next, my heart swelling more than I ever thought possible. "As far as I'm concerned, each of you will be this little one's father, and he or she will be the luckiest and most loved child on earth."

"He or she?" Dutch asked, looking around. "I think she meant *he*."

"Actually, I think she meant *she*," Christian said, laughing. "This place could use a little more feminine touch, let's face it."

I raised my hand before a huge debate erupted. "Who cares! All that matters is that we're a family."

As soon as Red set me down, Christian picked me up in his arms. "Well, we're not the typical sort of family."

Thank god for that.

"I wouldn't have it any other way."

EPILOGUE

THE MIDWIFE PLACED AN, angry, screaming, slippery, but beautiful little girl on Mari's chest. At least we'd been allowed to help a little.

Our girl, Mari. She held it together better than the rest of us. We, who were crying almost as much as our new baby.

Our baby.

I liked the sound of that.

We guys had been through hell and back together, and still bore the scars of some of the shit we'd seen and done.

We'd always harbor those scars.

But they seemed a lot less burdensome now that Mari was part of our family. She was making new memories with us, having come along just when we thought the movies running in our heads were what we'd have to watch for the rest of our lives.

They'd never be completely gone, but they surely would be replaced by finer remembrances. Like watching a beautiful little girl come into the world.

Cripes, our little princess was going to be spoiled. Four doting daddies? Hell, she didn't stand a chance, and neither did we.

Would we raise her on Savage Mountain? Or relocate somewhere where she'd be around other kids?

That remained to be seen. The only thing certain was our commitment to her and her mother.

Everything else would fall into place, someday, somehow.

We stood beside Mari's bed. Watching her filled our hearts as she took a deep breath, and offered our daughter a breast to nurse, quieting her naturally.

She made us better men by calming us, too. Centering us. Loving us.

I brushed a hair off her forehead, and ran my fingertips over her shoulder to touch my baby for the first time. I would have liked to stay like this forever, in a place that felt like a dream, where everything seemed possible, and where there was always a happy ending.

I bent to kiss both my loves on the tops of their heads.

We sure as hell didn't know what the future held for us, but we all had each other, and that was a perfect start.

DID YOU LIKE *The Runaway?*
Learn about the next book in the collection,
THE PURSUED

I hope you loved reading this book as much as I
loved writing it.
Find all Mika Lane books here:
https://mikalaneshop.com/

Dear Reader:

I'm USA TODAY bestselling romance author Mika Lane, and am OBSESSED with bringing you sassy, steamy stories with imperfect heroines and the bad-a*s dudes they bring to their knees. I'll always bring you my signature humor and heat, topped off with a modern-day happily ever after.

My first book ever was *The Day I Ate the Milkyway,* a true fourth-grade masterpiece illustrated with crayons and bound with construction paper and glue. Nowadays, steamy romance gives purpose to my days and nights as I create worlds and characters that tickle the imagination. I live in magical Northern California with my own handsome alpha dude, sometimes known as Mr. Mika Lane, and two devilish cats named Chuck and Murray.

A dual citizen of the United States and Ireland, I have on more than one occasion spent my last dollar on a plane ticket somewhere, and am always planning my next escape. I often try new recipes on unsuspecting friends, search out hiding places to read undisturbed, and sadly kill every houseplant I bring home.

I LOVE to hear from readers when I'm not dreaming up naughty tales to share. Visit my online shop https://mikalaneshop.com/ and say hello https://mikalaneshop.com/pages/meet-mika.

xoxo, Mika

www.ingramcontent.com/pod-product-compliance
Lightning Source LLC
Chambersburg PA
CBHW071142180726
48291CB00007B/2306